Turn
Points

by
Dermot Foster

'The turning points of lives are not the great moments. The real crises are often concealed in occurrences so trivial in appearance that they pass unobserved.'

—George Washington

Culture Matters promotes cultural democracy.
www.culturematters.org.uk

Edited by Mike Quille
Text © Dermot Foster
Cover Image © Dermot Foster
Typeset by Alan Morrison
ISBN 978-1-912710-60-7

Contents

Introduction

When you consider that these short stories have appeared very slowly and intermittently over a number of years you might assume that they are likely to be random and unrelated. Are they linked at all? Well, it's true that there are a few minor cross-references between the stories, but are they connected in a more significant way? What, if anything, do they hold in common? Have they managed to coalesce into a coherent collection?

The most notable feature common to every story is that there are turning points in the lives of the main characters—turning points in terms of a change in attitude, outlook and behaviour. In all the stories these turning points are quite slight and subtle, when seen from a broad ideological perspective, but they are discernible.

They are often hardly noticeable to the characters themselves, at the time they occur. For example, in **On the Move with Ron and Frank**, the eponymous drifters acknowledge that a primary school visit to a lemonade factory made one morning many years ago proved to be a formative experience in shaping their future adult lives.

Highly personal, everyday experiences, such as meeting a new person, or hearing a thoughtful comment made by a friend, can stimulate a shift or turning point, akin perhaps to a train gliding over points and altering its direction of travel. In **Put Out To Sea**, the initial series of tiny turning points happens on the spur of the moment when a student helps a young mum in the launderette. Changes follow for both of them and become highly significant and substantial for the latter in an upturn in her political consciousness. A hesitant, simple offer to go and watch a young man play cricket hints at a potential turning point at the conclusion of **The Careless Fielder.**

All of the stories in *Turning Points* have this in common: they are concerned with the microscopic level at which change does or doesn't happen for individuals—the mundane moments, moves and infant steps that can start to alter a person's outlook.

Socialism and progressive ideas and action could be said to grow from out of the gradual but vast accumulation of these countless individual turning points. Seeds are planted, and what then takes root may depend on what opportunities there are for support and solidarity. We can and do influence others, sometimes in a strange way as in **In Memory**, but not only by haranguing and constant campaigning, worthy though this may be at times.

In fact, a radical evangelical approach can be counterproductive, for various reasons. In the story **In Transit** we can see that it is the quiet, persistent personal example of acceptance of the travelling community by the art teacher rubbing off on Norman, the teaching assistant, that garners his support.

Individuals need to have a degree of open-mindedness to be receptive to change, to develop and mature. Although the main character in **Sanctuary** has had to make a radical turn in response to the most acute demands, the main concern of the story is how others respond to his bold action. In the tale **Trouble in Store** we're told that Berin has been nudged into volunteering to respond to the needs of the homeless on the streets, so has made that turn, only to find his relationship with Mr Choudrey very perplexing. What should he do next?

The narrator in **Battle for Bogside** is, by the end of the story, unsure what he feels about a schoolmate who mysteriously turns his back on his peers and takes a direction none of the others would ever think of following. Why indeed do some individuals keep a closed mind, and seem to be lacking in sympathy or empathy? Is it a failure of an individual's imagination, upbringing and socialisation? Or is it a result of broader, more dominant power structures in capitalist societies? Those are questions for psychologists and political theorists...or perhaps some further stories.

Speaking Out

'I've lost one of my feet.'

'What are you talking about?...How many do you have? When did you last see it?!'

'I can't find the one that holds...it's gone...Harry don't just sit there...come over and give me a hand, I'm dropping this. Harry! Now!'

'All these body parts...you want a hand to find a foot?!'

'I can't hold on much longer...the pot...it's going to tip over on me...please!'

Harry Bowen scraped back his chair and left me to continue sipping tea in his palm house of a conservatory while he sauntered over to assist his wife in her search. I noticed that it was a splendid shrub she was grimly holding onto and attempting to shift.

It had been a strange day, beginning with the malarkey of standing around outside Bowen's yard in town hoping to be picked out for a day's work. I always adopted my most upright posture, the one my Mum constantly asked for but seldom saw, in order to impress the supervisors selecting the crews. I would also try to stand close behind a shorter man, both as a height contrast trick but also to conceal my skinniness. The other tactic I employed was an attempt to achieve a balance between looking keen and energetic without appearing desperate. It was quite a hard part for me to perform and I had failed the audition this morning. Not selected to make up one of the four or five work crews employed to erect or dismantle Bowen marquees on hire all over the East Midlands meant no pay day today.

However, Mr Bowen, hanging about in the wings, had come centre stage and told me that I could spend the day at his place deep in the Leicestershire countryside.

'It's a fine house, a former nunnery. Costs a fortune to maintain.'

We had sped away in his new top of the range car, air-conditioning full on. Arriving in next to no time, he had then instructed me to weed his impressively long drive, providing only a hoe, shovel and wheelbarrow. Guessing correctly that I was unfamiliar with the use of these implements, he had briefly demonstrated how to use the hoe efficiently and then left me there to develop blisters and sunstroke for what seemed hours until eventually summoning me for this tea break at midday.

Over a cuppa and a digestive biscuit he had presented me with his view on why Ted Heath was the right man to take control of the country, how the unions were ruining everything and why we should go into the Common Market. I guessed he wasn't interested in what I might have to say as he never paused long enough for me to respond. I was glad in a way as I wouldn't have known where to start.

The following day had been better as I had been selected to join a gang led

1

by Steve.

'Hey what do you know, we're off to a friggin' pop festival site. They've said I can take Frank...now he's available!'

Steve announced this to the two of us crammed in the cabin of the pick-up van with him. He was excited and accelerated hard.

'You know I always speed through these Pakki streets...see if I can't clip any of the buggers...or at least get 'em to jump!'

He appeared to be aiming to do exactly that as two sedate ladies of East African Indian origin glided across the street in their gilded saris taking tiny unseen steps. I felt scared and then relieved when he missed them by a whisker. When he droned on spewing out examples of his warped thinking, well, I felt numb and nauseous. But I said nothing, simply stared ahead, keeping still, hoping he'd shut up and not invite me to contribute.

In the middle of Loughborough's largest council estate, we drew up outside Frank's house. There was a milk crate by the front door overflowing with empty beer and spirit bottles.

Steve explained:' We had a lot to celebrate...'specially Frank.'

'Was it his birthday?' I asked. Steve's had responded with a withering look. The door opened. We were all invited in, mugs of tea reeking of whisky thrust into our hands. When Frank came out with us to the van, I wondered how the four of us would fit in the cab.

So there I was on the flat-bed of the pick-up, sitting with my legs splayed out, my back hard against the cab determined to avoid rolling anywhere near the non-existent sides, only able to stare back at the wake, the motorway streaming away, and holding on as best I could. On my right side was a box strapped down. I squeezed a hand in through the strap though it was a tight fit. On the other side I found that when the truck swerved in one direction I could press on to a part of the cab which stuck out slightly. I had had to concentrate whilst Steve steamed down the M1 the truck bobbing about, lurching forward at every opportunity to overtake. Even on one occasion undertaking, using the hard shoulder, and meant that a coachload of surprised passengers gawped down at me, many with startled eyes and slack mouths. I felt their looks expressed both shock and pity.

The festival site shook us. As far as the eye could see across the deserted muddy stretches of flattened fields was litter and devastation. Small heaps of waste, large deposits of rubbish. We spread out, searching everywhere for Mr Bowen's precious marquees. All that could be located after half an hour, was torn strips of marque or tent material scattered over a large area, and the two main poles like masts from a stricken ship, slightly charred in places. The rigging or ropes were cut up here and there. The only gear completely intact was of course the pegs. When you worked for Bowen's these were referred to as the 'pins' although each weighed about three or four pounds and seemed to be cast-iron. How my arms had ached for a couple of days when I was first asked to fetch half a dozen.

We were informed informally that matters had got a bit out of hand at the festival with torrential weather and a help yourself approach adopted when the storm was at its height.

'They all want locking up or putting in the sodding army!' declared Steve.

I too felt upset, but didn't know quite what to say. I'd been to festivals. It had been great, the vibes far out. At the last one we'd helped a bit to clear the site whilst also keeping a look out for souvenirs in a beachcombing way. I couldn't articulate this and anyway Steve was stomping about deciding which washed-up Bowen fragments to load onto the truck. In all it seemed a pitiful amount given the fifty mile return journey.

We never learnt how Mr Bowen had reacted. Having tipped out the remnants towards the back of the depot, we scarpered, but later heard it said that the insurance would see Owen's well looked after.

'What the...when did this become no entry,' shouted Frank, who was now driving, at no-one in particular as he pressed on through the town centre. We had dropped off the others and were returning to HQ.

'It's been like this a few months...part of the re-designed one-way system.'

'Well...they could have bloody well told me. Well...it would have been hard to I suppose where I were... been away most of the year see.' I didn't see at all what point he was making, but thought it best not to enquire. In fact tucked-up in my middle-class cocoon I only came to add two and two together a couple of months later.

Next day it was audition time again and I was pleased that Steve beckoned me over before the supervisor could choose. He wanted me in his crew. I supposed that he liked the fact that I was very quiet, compliant, not likely to mutiny.

He and the supervisor then quickly picked out another young man. I could see why they had chosen Nick. We covered a broad range of ages, elderly teens like myself right through to old rather decrepit lags who you would have thought were pensioners. Nick was early twenties and heavily muscled and looking for holiday work. He cut a dashing D'Artagnan figure with his tumbling locks hanging over his shoulders, his twirly moustache and leather waistcoat. It was soon very clear that Nick was not unknown to Steve.

'How's the Jean of my dreams Nick? Still shacked up with that bolshie git? You still stuck in Wilberforce Road with all our colonial cousins?'

'Dave's all right. I like him...and Mum's happy now. They've put a little

3

extension on the back and, it's only about two minutes' walk to work...so it suits them fine.'

'Oh ay. I hear lover boy is a shop steward at Tootles.'

'Senior shop steward actually!'

'Yea. Makes sure all the Pakis get the easy and best paid work then.'

'Oh come on. You know it's not like that. Anyway they're not Pakistanis ...they're Indian...Ugandan Asians and British citizens...'

'Yea, right...well, he's welcome to them. I was so bloody glad to get out.'

I listened attentively. I could, I was in the cab as we were a three man gang on a short run to haul in a small marquee from a fancy wedding do at a posh house. Nick and Steve continued to converse back and forth about the relative merits of immigration. Not that Steve saw any positives, thought Nick was deluded, and clearly felt threatened. I was impressed at how well Nick could remain so calm meeting what were waves of offensive utterances from Steve. He explained, provided cogent facts, revealed the contradictions in Steve's thinking, cajoled him and practically pleaded with him to be simply less prejudiced and more open minded. Was he planting any seeds of change in Steve's head I wonder?

'There's lots that agree with me you know. We're the silent majority.' Steve was often heard to mutter.

We three were together all the following day too, sitting around in the cab with Nick while Steve had gone off in search of fags and, we suspected, a couple of quick pints. I praised Nick for his standing up to Steve yesterday.

'Not that I got anywhere...but why don't you do the same...we've got to challenge these bigots? The more of us the better.'

'I know. I should. I want to...I would feel better...but I find I get wound up... and anyway he's more likely to take it from you. He just sees me as another middle-class do-gooder not living anywhere near immigrant areas and just getting all the benefits...'

'That's a cop out! It may be an uphill struggle in the short term but...' Nick was eloquent as usual and spoke at length. I was quiet, nodded a lot, but finally could only shrug. I even stayed away from Bowen's for a few days but bumped into Nick one night in the Crown and Mitre. He was pleased to see me.

'No more lectures, mate, I promise. You should come back...you know Bowen has even upped our pay by two bob an hour. Bit short of staff apparently. My mate Majid's coming down tomorrow...you'd like him...he's a good laugh.'

I was somewhat surprised next morning to see so few waiting at Bowen's to be hired. Clearly the pay rise hadn't had the desired impact our Harry had been hoping for.

I had a word with a new guy who had turned up as I knew he must be Majid. He said Nick had twisted his ankle and could only hobble about. A few minutes later, I was completely baffled when we were all quickly taken on, except for Majid. He alone was left to slope off after consoling me that it was nothing to fret about and he'd come back when Nick was fit to work again.

He had been politely informed, by way of a quiet word, it seems, that he was unfortunately surplus to requirements at this moment in time. This was odd as Steve and I were sent on a lengthy job collecting two marquees.

Tired, we returned late that evening to the depot and after twenty minutes of unloading and storing Steve left. I was going out the door with them when I remembered my coat. As I returned to pick up my discarded jacket I spotted Mr Bowen locking up the office. I continued my departure, but stopped half-way across the yard to retrieve a pen that had fallen out of a pocket. I noticed that he was climbing into his Jag. The security lights had been triggered in the evening gloom and we were floodlight, if anyone cared to watch. He looked up, saw me and smiled, saying:

'Do me a favour please, I'm in a hurry, let me go through first and...make sure the yard gate locks behind you on your way out.'

In reply I blurted out:

'Ok, but do you know why Majid was not taken on today?'

'The young Asian guy you mean...well, it's none of your business...'

'But we were short staffed...it took us a lot longer and we ran out of time to get over to help at Long Eaton and they're having to go back tomorrow and...'

'Look, I haven't got time to listen to you telling me how to run my business...the point is, if you must know...we don't employ Asians, not at this moment in time...I mean...I'd have a bloody mutiny on my hands if I did...my regulars wouldn't stand for it...I can't afford to be sentimental, son.'

I tried to argue with him. Unlike Nick, I found myself shouting.

Mr Bowen rapidly became exasperated. He thrust his hand through the car window, his fingers gunning straight at me and bluntly pointed out that I needn't bother looking for work at Bowen's any longer.

'Find somewhere else to take your bleeding heart. I don't have to explain to you how I choose to run my business. I don't take kindly to...look, I have taken the trouble to explain... And I'm still in a hurry...there's nothing more to say.'

Then he added: 'Run along now. Leave the gate...I'll make sure it's properly locked. Go on, scarper.'

On the Move With Ron and Frank

Ron and Frank were settled comfortably in the shade of two willow trees. They sprawled out on an old blanket, determined to retreat from the searing heat and their French mates from the commune. They could lie back now and watch them bustling about on board their barge, moored a few metres away. Not a narrowboat, Frank kept muttering, far too large to fit an English canal and squeeze through a lock.

They could hear singing, but it was coming from along the towpath. Glancing up from their manufacture of quality joints, they saw through the heat haze a portly gent on a bike wobbling towards them. His bike was not completely under his control, the balance was in doubt and the steering lamentable.

Ben gently applied the brakes and his steed stopped alongside them. He was staring at the vessel in front of him, bedecked with flags, bunting, pennants, Buddhist prayer wheels, huge psychedelic tie-dye banners, peace signs and zodiacs. Flowers overflowed, wisteria was winding all over the cabin and bougainvillaea ran rampant. Plants in pots crowded the deck, window boxes were stuffed with geraniums and bunches of dried flowers rested over the bows. A couple of dogs stretched out where they had found space underneath a hammock, amongst the bikes, camping chairs and children's toys.

'Holy Moses, will you look at that,' he blurted out. 'That's amazing!'

'Yea, but you should try living there, mate. With that lot,' Frank was stung into responding.

'Oh, hello...I didn't see you there...hiding here in the shade. You're English?'

'Yea, like yourself.'

'Well, I'm more Irish really as it happens...'

'Never mind. Somebody has to be, I suppose. Grab a seat man...over here, where it's cool...here on our blanket...you look like you need a rest. I'm Ron by the way and this here gent goes by the name of Frank.'

'Ah, don't mind if I do. Pleased to meet you. I am Ben. Listen, I've got some wine left...to go with your smokes fellas...and plenty of bread and cheese left... if you would care to partake.' He threw the bike over against the trunk in a dismissive manner and ferreted around in the panniers for the items.

'Ben man...lay all your burdens down...sink into the cool depths of these shadows...bliss out!'

Despite their prosaic names, Ben considered them rather exotic looking company what with their Cuban heels, bell-bottom pants, carefully embroidered below the knee with a 'v' shape extra flare, a piece of tapestry no less. They sported tight leather waistcoats with a paisley shirt for Ron and a denim one for Frank. Ron boasted a bountiful afro, Frank had flowing locks disappearing over his shoulders. Both had fancy beards and earrings and Ben thought of Frank as the Laughing Cavalier. Mind you, the cavaliers never wore neck chokers, or smoked dope, as far as he knew.

They were fascinated to learn from Ben that he was on a post-festival holiday.

'So, you are the main man...the head that gets it together for the Cheltn'm festival. Who was on this year, Ben?'

'Well...I doubt, not sure you'll know them, bit before your time perhaps... it's folk, jazz and blues mainly you see, with some stand-up performance poets thrown in...so to speak!'

'You mean heads that are clever with words... can juggle rhymes, do hand-stands spouting verse and...pull them Jap high cure thingies out of hats?' smirked Ron. 'Hey, but any soul food man...that's where it's at you know...soul music...so cool...can cure a lotta ills. Here cop some of this.' He held out his joint.

Ben, using all his diplomatic festival-negotiating skills, kindly turned down the offer of a toke.

'I'm a bit old for it lads...and not being a smoker...well, it would be wasted on me, but thanks.'

'That's ok...hey Frank, listen. Ben's a joke, a bloke who won't take a toke!' Ron giggled. 'I'm a poet, don't ya know it!'

'What do you do in the long winter months?' asked Frank.

'Well, whatever pays. Could be the cardboard packaging factory, or a few days on the Post at Christmas. I used to go back to Ireland to Mayo and do supply teaching or support work. I was a teacher once, you see...tiny school on Achill Island...only five or six pupils...lessons on the beach sometimes...until they closed us down.'

Ron now took up another line of enquiry. 'I noticed, Ben, that you weren't half unsteady on that bike of yours. I thought you were going to topple over.'

'Ah yes, my trusty mount is poorly, gone quite lame.'

'How do you mean?'

'Well, the front wheel is pretty crooked, and a bit loose, can't tighten it, back wheel also doesn't run true, chains gone quite rusty in places...I could go on...gears are mashed, also can't adjust the handlebars.'

'You're not selling it to me, man'. They all laughed. 'Best ditch it mate, me thinks.'

'Now there, you're not wrong. You're quite right.'

Languidly, an invitation emerged from Ron and Frank encouraging Ben to stop here for the night, on board. In the morning he might join them hitching north towards Germany or Belgium.

'It's high time we split,' announced Frank. 'We don't ever want to be tied down. Our French friends here talk of moving down south but won't raise the anchor. We reckon they'll end up staying over winter...they're always hopping over there to the village.' Ben could see that Frank was pointing to buildings a couple of fields away. 'They've even started talking about the kids going to school.'

'We know one of them...Evy, from our time in a squat in Brixton see. Didn't reckon on her as the settling-down type mind,' explained Ron.

'Not a bad thing surely? Best of both worlds, Ron?'

'No...well, what we want is... to see beyond that Ben...beyond the beyond... set no limits, man!'

Evy had whispered to him while he was helping her clear away the dishes and debris from the evening meal. 'Our English friends, they don't...I think they are sweet boys, but they think they are on holiday here. All the time. We have work to do...they like to holiday.'

Ben opted to kip on deck in a hammock suspended beneath the stars, Hendrix echoing around the heavens and after the music faded, the occasional gentle lapping of water.

In the morning Ben swopped his rusty bike for a musty rucksack that Evy dug out. They would repair the bike, perhaps, she thought. Ben had the most useful items from his panniers packed into the rucksack, which he swung over his back as the three companions ambled off in search of lifts.

The hitching, when they at last found a road going north, was hard work in the baking sunshine. Only thirty kilometres achieved, in the two hours of hitching it took to reach Chaumont.

'You got any bread, man ...no not that...no, sorry, I mean dosh, Ben?'

They mustered quite a few francs between them with Frank squirming about in his pants and then squeezing out some notes from his secret inside pocket sewn into his trousers. 'Couldn't be too careful down in Provence with that lot picking grapes. Pick your pocket as well. We liked it though, aim to come back.'

'Have you ever gone apple harvesting in England?'

'No, Ben, never...it's an idea.'

Settling on a bench in a park overlooking the pretty town, munching delicious grub, they indulged in idle chat. The sun was dappled by trees.

Ben sighed. 'Ah, but this is a joy! This is the life, isn't it?'

'Here Frank...Ben likes poetry...you got that poem, that quote. You remember you wrote it down...see Ben it was painted on the side of this barge. Passed by us the other day with all these heads on board. They stopped to chat to our French friends. They were going down south for the winter.'

'Oh, yea. Hang on a mo Ron...oh, here it is...I keep it handy. We dig it. He who bends...bends? Shit... I can't see...can't read me own writing. Uh, no. It's He who binds...binds is better. He who binds to himself a joy...does the winged life destroy, but, he who kisses the joy as it flies, lives in eternity's sunrise. Good innit, rhymes an' all. Heavy. Who wrote...?'

'Ah yes indeed...Billy Blake that is...you know, William Blake,' answered Ben. 'He wanted the wing-ed life...'

'Wing-ed life, right...see those losers who say they can't wait to leave school, get a job in the factory, 'cause at fifteen they reckon they'll be earning big time...that joy don't last long...maybe a couple of months,' muttered Ron.

'None of my business Ron, but how come you left that art college?'

Before Ron can say a word, Frank exclaims, 'He's a born rebel, this one, you see. Never liked no-one telling him what not to do, what to do...always a right to do if they did...proper little anarchist...even back in bloody nursery school...always in trouble, this fella.'

'Frank's exaggerating of course. It's true I suppose that...uh...well, I find it a heavy scene... don't like authority. See they had this occupation at college. Threw out the straights...the ones in charge and I thought great, but...well, the student leaders said yippy we're having us a revolution...what a joke...tried to run the place...with a bit of help from a few hip teachers. The leaders thought they...thought it was mind-blowing or summat...who were they kidding, and when they started telling me what I should be doing and studying...it was a bunch of middle-class white kids power-playing...it was the final straw.'

'See what I mean, he don't take bullshit from no one, our Ron!'

'But couldn't you join in, have your say? Weren't decisions democratic...'

'Yea, but these bossy student sods Ben were thinking them the ones could run everything...they know best. None of 'em listened to me an' I was the only black bro there...in the entire place...think they would've ask me...but they never did...still...they's what they call it, top of the heap...the Man still in charge. A hierarchy, ain't it?'

'Talking of decisions,' Frank butt in, 'we need to split up or it's goin' to take weeks to hitch home. You know how it works Ben... two birds get a ride dead quick, then a bloke and a bird, then a bloke on his lonesome, then two blokes... any road, three blokes with massive rucksacks is asking too much.'

'Yea, pity...but you're right. Three's a crowded 2CV. We might meet up further on. In case we don't, here's my address near Cheltenham. Keep it with your William Blake.'

'How about you Frank?'

'Whatcha mean?'

'How did you come to this way of living?'

'You mean, just groovin' around? Now that's...I dunno, I never thought about it so as to explain it to anyone...it just suits me I suppose...well, I suppose it goes back...suppose I knew what I didn't want. When me and him was at junior school, ten or so we'd be...we had this trip to visit a local place of work...part of our education, or indoctrination Ron now says...we went to a lemonade factory.'

'My uncle worked there, remember Frankie? Only bleeding job he could get...nobody else would look at him. We kids thought it sounded great.'

'Yea, that's right. What gave us the heebie-jeebies was watching mesmerised while this bloke, poor bugger, sat by this conveyor belt all day...and all he had to do was screw the tops on every bottle tight, or check they was on right tight...on every single bottle going past. Didn't even get to put the bleeding tops on himself. Just tighten them up. All day. Today! Yesterday! Tomorrow! Forever. Screw that for a life is what we say!'

Ron took up the theme. 'Factory work...it's all the same, innit? Can be good money I grant you, but it would drive us right round the friggin' bend! My old man says one or two of the lads he knows shot up to Halewood, you know the new car plant at Liverpool. Tried Dagenham, nothing doing. Lasted only two months up there. Desperate for good money, but the line goes twice as fast up there when it started. They were taking the piss cause they're all new to it, them Scousers...trying it on there...till unions got to sort 'em out.'

'We like to be doing anything that gets us out and about. We dig seeing different places. Drifting along...meeting people.'

So shortly after they returned to England, they went to check out Ben's base near Cheltenham. They found his HQ was a rented caravan in a barn at a farm owned and run by a family he was friendly with. He enjoyed working on the farm when other work was not forthcoming, and having encouraged Ron and Frank to try their hand at harvesting apples, Ben was not too surprised in early October to see them mooching up the drive into the farmyard, in their Cuban heels.

'Good timing, gents. Tom will show you round. Tell him you can start as soon as he wants you. He's looking to start any day now. This will save him recruiting. Here, let me show you one of the other caravans... your luxury accommodation, should you choose to stay...with its 50s décor. It's ancient, bit draughty, but watertight and the barn's quite warm.'

Apples were to be carefully unscrewed from their tenuous hold on the twigs and branches of the orchard trees. If fallen and maggoty, collected for animal food. So many, such a burden for the poor bent trees to carry.

'We're doing them a favour, Ben,' Frank suggested.

'Yea, a mercy,' Ron added.

'It's of mutual benefit surely, Ron?'

'Yea. If only it lasted longer. We'll be finished in another three or four days, according to the gaffer. He may have one or two bits of work for us to do he said but nothing long term.'

'Time to move on then? Not easy in the winter. There's a lot of hotel work round here or in restaurants. Oh, and possibly Mrs Campbell.'

'Yea, maybe. Hey, tell us about this Luther bloke Ben...your American buddy. Those mates of yours in the pub last night seemed keen to know how he's doing. Who is he?'

'Long story Ron. Ok I'll tell you a little...he's safe now. He was a draft dodger I met three years back. Black guy from Harlem. Only nineteen. Played in a combo at the festival. I did what I could...he's in Sweden now, we got him out. Unbelievably good sax player...no call for that in Vietnam. He'd done one tour, wasn't going again that's for sure, not after what he'd seen...the napalm, agent orange, the chopper raids on villages...listen, not a word about it, please. Hey how you enjoying it here, the apple picking, sticking your ladders towards heaven still?'

'What, you what?'

'Oh, that's a bit of Robert Frost...another poet. Luther liked that poem. Liked it here in the orchards. I meant to say, you know with the apples finishing, you're looking for something else, well, as I say, there's Mrs Campbell's business in town. Tom says she's maybe looking for people. Anyhow that's what she told him to tell me.'

'Pity we can't just hibernate here in the barn and crawl out in the spring,' Ben added.

Ben also suggested that there was often work to be had with the market traders, usually setting up and clearing away, not regular and it meant very early starts, but puts a few quid in your pocket plus trips to neighbouring towns for their market days.

Frank found gainful employment after a couple of weeks working in a small industrial unit a mile away, Mrs Campbell's company, which supplied posh wool and woollen clothing to customers. Casual work, agreed on a weekly arrangement, Mrs Campbell had hastened to add. Temporary work to cover the increase of orders up to Christmas which would tide him over for some of the worst of winter. There were six of them in the warehouse, dealing with shipments arriving and completing orders to post out. It was routine, of limited interest rather than numbskull boring. The 'remuneration', as the boss called it, was not quite as poor as he had anticipated and he could put up with it for a while, especially as Tom charged very little rent for use of their snug van in the barn.

However, after a few weeks an unexpected snag emerged. Mrs Campbell said she needed to see him in her office. She wanted a quiet word. For some strange reason she wanted to know about his father.

'He's from London, isn't he?'

'Me ol' man?' Frank half grinned in a perplexed way. 'Why him?'

'Is he a brickie from London, Dagenham?'

'That's right. How did you know? Why do you want...'

'Ok. What's his name?'

'Hey?' A long pause before Frank gave the simple answer the question required.

'Well...it's Francis, actually. Why?'

'Right...that's him then. We thought...now a little bird tells me that Francis Cooper is a known troublemaker...big time. Stirs up, agitates. Big on unions, isn't he?'

'Oh that. Yea. Some say that...but that's unfair and it's got nothin' to do with me. I don't know...'

'Listen. I happen to know he works around on building sites and deliberately tries to foment trouble. Gets the others to join his union. Demand more pay. Push everybody out for a strike. Hold the company to ransom.'

'Oh I dunno 'bout that. But anyway...that's not me.'

'But you were overheard yesterday making remarks about getting your union to come to your aid. I don't know what union...'

'I was only joking...What union anyway? I was just shooting my mouth off. It don't mean nothing...it's just a bit of banter...you know when someone says...you ought to get your union on to that. I know there's no...'

'Well. I'm not having it. Not a Frank Cooper on any payroll of mine. You'll have to go at the end of the week and find somewhere else to make your wisecracks. Can't have any of that sort of talk here.' Frank started to defend himself again, but she just stared him down whilst pointing to the door.

He slunk back home to the barn and sank a can of beer. Then stepped out over to Ben's van. Ben was clearly put out by his news, but said that he wasn't totally surprised. Very disappointed in someone he considered a friend. Well a friend of the festival.

'Claimed I'm some sort of union agitator who wants to bring her business down, your Mrs C.'

'Very sorry to hear that Frank...I did hear that she's looking to expand, take on more staff...even open a new base in Shrewsbury or Bristol. Obviously super sensitive...concerned with keeping down costs, keeping pay low...way over the top this though...I blame that fool of a husband, the house builder, big developer he is round here...he's scared her...he's scared stiff of unions

15

and hates regulations...a bore on the subject...they reckon he cuts corners... there's been some stuff in the local rag about trouble on building sites across the county...listen Frank...if you want, I'll have a word, see if I can sort it. Can't promise...can't promise to change her mind.'

'That's kind Ben, but don't bother. If she's like that it'll only happen again... and soon. You did say, some time ago, that she's a big supporter of your festival, getting her...whatsits...'

'Yea, Round Table chums involved. She likes to be seen supporting the community and the arts...mind you she's starting to cool it anyway...muttering about too many long-haired degenerates taking part...I thought she was better than this though Frank...it's got to be her old man getting to her ...so sorry.'

Ron joined them and heard Frank's sad little tale.

'Hey Frank, maybe it's just as well. Listen, I can't see my market boy act carrying on much longer. Time to move on man...the retail industry will just have to manage without me. Bit of a bummer but...don't look so upset Ben. You've been a mate and we can come back next year...there'll always be another apple harvest.'

'Yea Ron's right...the joy's gone here...it must have flown somewhere else for us...we could find it by moving on though.'

'But don't you fellows ever feel like settling down, make a home? Put down some roots? Don't you get tired always having to move on, be at someone's beck and call? Must you always be hard travelling?'

'My Dad used to get mad at me...when I told him I wasn't hanging around stuck in a crap job. He used to say, well do summat 'bout it, stay an' fight 'em, get organised or they'll walk all over you. No, like Ron says, you know, we like moving on coz we can. We're only twenty-five you know, not thirty-five or forty-five! We can keep on trucking for a long time yet...anyhow Ben, you spend a fair amount of time groovin' around.'

'Well, yea, of course. I go away when I can. I'm not trapped here. But this is my retreat, I like to have a place to call home. I'm making a life here.'

'Ben the best-of-both-worlds, eh!' Ron smiled as he said this and then continued:

'I think you're always getting nearer by not keeping still...when you're on the move, I mean. We heard that from a hip guy we met once.'

'Hey, you're getting real heavy, man! There's no stopping Ron on a roll.'

'Nearer to what, Ron?' Ben wanted to know.

'Nearer to finding what we want I suppose...won't know till we get there... it's all about exploring...not freaking out when...well, sort of expecting to find the unexpected...oh, I don't know. You never know do you?...just leave the bad scenes behind man, that's the main thing. Anyway, it's been great knowing you Ben, but...'

Frank and Ron chorused, 'Time to move on.' Ron left them.

'Ron seems quite cheerful.'

'Well, it's because he went out to phone his old lady earlier...see how all his kids are doing...'

'What?! You joking?'

'Yea! He phoned an old girlfriend up in Manchester, not that she has any children...to see if it's a good time for us to crash at her place...and it is!'

Ben looked lost.

'No apples to harvest up there though!'

'True, but there's Eighth Day, with plenty of dishes to wash an' bread to bake.'

'Eighth Day? Why that name? What's that all about?'

'You know your Bible Ben, on the eighth day...well things really took off... it's a co-op café and we have mates there. It's like this...we have quite a few, what Ron calls, safe houses, you know, stopping off places where we can expect a warm welcome. It's Wales or Manky...could be back to Brixton if all else fails. Connections, man.'

'You sound like one of them old travellers, the Romany people, you know... with their traditional campsites strung out across the country...we had some-one give a talk couple of years ago...played some of the old songs as well.'

'Yea, it's the way to live. Way to go.'

Trouble in Store

‘I tell you, he was living there…in his storage unit or somebody's unit. I saw him! He was scuttling out of the toilet at the end of the corridor, clutching a spongebag…and a large towel.’

Steve had just ambled in from his lunchtime stroll around the surrounding streets This had included nipping into the medieval Cheetham's library. He hung up his jacket and listened in.

Anju was fielding questions from her colleagues in an excitable voice, barely giving herself time to draw breath.

‘Yea, they have this large disabled toilet, oh, you know…I mean…toilet and shower room which can cater for the needs of people with dis…’

‘But where does he actually live?’, someone butted in. ‘How can he live in a steel cupboard Anj? Must be horrible…doesn't bear thinking about.’

‘Well, they're not exactly cupboards you know…more like…tiny rooms without windows…about…two metres by about three and they're open to the roof and it's a huge hangar-type place…I don't know what the CCTV coverage is like but they do bang on about it being extensive…’

Steve, wanting to make his presence felt, lobbed in a comment : ‘Perhaps he's made a little den, well away from prying eyes…a little hideout. Oh it sounds quite cute!’

Anju ignored Steve's flippancy and continued. ‘Anyway, I was told by Francis in Housing that she has heard from someone that this sort of thing is happening, I mean that people are finding all sorts of alternative living places. It's not surprising really, when you think about it…I mean look at the number of people sleeping rough right here in the city centre. Look outside this building!’

Two phones began ringing in the office – united in their attempt to remind the team that they ought to be working on sorting out the legal complexities and compliance demands faced by Manchester City Council. Steve's desk adjoined Anju's, but neither phone was ringing for them, so Anju asked Steve to report on his lunch break. She wanted steering away from her unsettling experience.

‘At least you're not storing it up…you're getting it out of your system! Sorry, only joking. Don't look like that. I see now it has upset you. Anyway, at Chets Library they really do push the Marx Engels association. They are so proud of it, but it did feel a bit too much like a pilgrimage…the Chinese apparently…’

‘Hey, I thought you would have liked all that and would want to see where the guys got it together. Didn't you say once that it was the maternity unit of the manifesto!’

Steve grinned. ‘Now don't go all cynical on me, or Karl.’

'Or Friedrich. Yes, well, I can at least speak with some authority on this, unlike you...remember I grew up as a child in a strong Naxalite community. I tell you it was scary hearing the comrades talk, reading the slogans on the wall, and then waiting for the authorities to do what they always threatened to do.'

What was that?'

'To wipe us out, of course!' They were always arresting people and then you could never find out what had happened to them and in fact it wasn't a good idea to even ask anyone. When I say 'arrested' them it wasn't like here. They declared a State of Emergency you know and then used it as a cover for torture, imprisonment without trial and...oh, the usual totalitarian crimes.'

'Apart from provoking the authorities then, what did these Naxalites do exactly? Were they a more moderate version of Naxals? No, sorry, only joking again...so how did your family view them?'

'We all thought they were ok, seriously...they were good guys, what was not to like?...they turned out to help when you needed help...say you were in trouble with a landlord, or needed food or money in an emergency...or wanted to go on strike but needed support. They also had literacy classes as well as political teaching. The government said they were worse than the mafia, that they terrorised communities, brainwashed children...you name it!'

Anju was renowned in the office for her steady, firm grip when faced with what their managers tended to refer to as 'challenges' rather than what were for staff stressful problems. Now her damp eyes appeared to show a state of both excitement and anxiety. At a hasty mid-afternoon break, she admitted to Steve that she was still thinking about the man hiding away in storage.

'I suppose it's a bit like a stowaway...except the ship's not going anywhere,' she suggested.

'What was he like?'

'You mean, was he a cool white hipster or a frightened little Asian rabbit?' Steve smiled. 'Well...give me some idea. A picture.'

'Ok. A miniature! He was Asian. He was small, dark and probably Bengali or Bangledeshi. I suppose that's why I keep thinking about him. He seemed familiar in some way I can't put my finger...I can't work it out.'

A few days later, the storage man as she called him, was still playing games in her head as she described it, scampering along corridors in her mind. She asked Steve for a favour. She wanted him to accompany her to her self-storage unit. Her cousin, she said, was soon to start university and was to be given or loaned a variety of items from her store, including a little bookcase, a few books, a lot of empty files, a reading lamp and some small rugs.

'There's not a huge amount to carry, but...'

'You want me to play the teenage Hollywood, or is it Bollywood, male carrying your books and accompanying you safely home.'

'I know, it's a bit pathetic, especially as you have quite a grey beard and a lovely wife and two sweet children at home!'

'No problem, as the young say all the time these days...you know when you go into a coffee shop, as they call them these days, and ask for a coffee and they say...'

'No worries...We could go tomorrow lunch, if that's ok , and I'll treat you to a mezze today!'

Steve agreed, but suggested a taxi back in view of the time-scale. Her cousin and his Dad no doubt would come in with Anju and collect the retrieved goods from the office on Saturday, she thought.

'It occurs to me though that if you are getting a taxi back you don't really need any help, do you? I mean I am more than happy to...and I like a walk with a purpose...oh, I see, you are worried about coming across that stowaway again!'

Anju nodded, slightly.

When they reached the massive security fence, the huge gate was wide open with a van coming out and they followed someone else walking in. The front doors opened automatically into a large lobby with a reception area to one side if you needed to ask any questions, raise any concerns. Going straight ahead at the inner door, Anju punched in a code. Now they were inside the hangar housing nearly two hundred units and took the lift to the second floor.

In the lift, as the floor button was being pushed and as the doors clanged shut, a man burst in to join them. They were taken aback as there had been no sign of anyone else around. He was short and stared up at them. He had what looked like a little map of India tattooed on his right cheek, an ink stain of a birth mark. It even featured a Sri Lankan blob. When the second floor was reached, the lift lurched briefly and Anju's ID badge swung forward. Their lift mate instinctively shot out a hand to stop the badge striking him and ended up holding on to it. Just as it appeared that he might yank her over towards him, he dropped the badge as if it were red hot and flustering gabbled out:

'I see...you work for council...I would like if you help me?'

'We're on a break from work at the moment, mate,' Steve suggested.

Anju motioned the man to step out of the lift ahead of them.

'My friend, he look for somewhere to live. Most urgent, you see...nowhere to live...nowhere to live anywhere. Impossible...the situation you see...great need of help, my friend.'

He darted glances, not just at them, but up and down the corridor with its endless sequence of steel doors and white blank breeze block walls. Steve and

Anju looked at each other, both thinking that they knew the answer to the next question, but feeling that they had to ask it anyway.

Steve went first: 'Where is your friend living now?'

'Oh, he is in tent poor man...in the arches...you know by big library, near council hall, in the big square. Many live there with him.'

They both looked a little more relieved than perhaps they felt they ought to hearing this reply..

'Yes, it's shocking,' Anju muttered after a moment, 'where some people end up living.'

As quickly as they could, the two experienced professionals established the relevant facts concerning this man's friend and offered reasonable, practical if general advice and then insisted that they had urgent business of their own to which they needed to attend and moved off down the corridor.

They just about had time to hear a thank you as they turned smartly and moved away around the corner. As Anju fiddled with her padlock, her hands trembling, Steve asked:

'Do you think that was the guy...you know...the one you saw...never mind his story about a mate in a tent?'

'I don't know Steve...could be. I didn't see his face clearly before...I can't be sure. And, anyway...well, how would someone get in here...you know...if they haven't got a unit? How?'

'Oh, as it happens I was asking Phil from security the other day that very question. He says it's a piece of cake...child's play sort of thing. You saw that large van when we came in...small businesses use these places a lot...often hire removal firms for a day or so and they often use casual staff...it's pretty common...any so-called security codes they have here will be widely shared... easily available. Maybe our friend was tipped off by someone he knows who worked a bit moving stuff in or out. Phil did say you could also...if you know who to contact...pay for the information. He said probably half the inmates in Strangeways would know...exaggeration of course and the storage people will update the numbers from time to time.'

'Makes me want to get an even heavier padlock...'

*

The following morning, Anju was surprised to be buzzed by reception. A Mr Choudrey had an appointment to see her. Right now.

'I don't have any such appointment, but I'll come down and try to get shot of him for you.' Anju had sensed that the man met in the storage place might try to cross her path again and had sought advice in order to be prepared.

She managed to dispatch Mr Choudrey, after noting his full name, whilst deploying considerable amounts of professional charm, kept in reserve for just such an occasion. Sufficient eye-contact was made to appear kind and considerate, she felt, and she was sure that she managed to sound reasonable when firing off the key messages from her notes, supplied by a very experienced colleague. She tried to make the bullets points sound less brisk and eminently achievable. Towards the conclusion of the process, without touching him, she inched him over towards the automatic door which opened onto St Peter's Square. He took an age to move forward far enough to trigger its opening. There might have been a hint of desperation in her closing remark: 'Good luck and goodbye'.

He crept out. She turned away swiftly, but glancing back, at the foot of the door to her stairs, she saw him standing stock still studying the leaflets she had supplied. Giant cranes were working silently behind him on the far side of the square in which a bright yellow tram slid across acres of new posh stone flagging. Before she stole out of the public lobby a last look made her wonder if anything she had said had registered with him.

*

At the Diwali party, organised as always by her mother, Anju's cousin Berin was thanking her again for the psychology books, bookcase, rugs, reading lamp and the various other items she had lent him which, she was impressed, he could list far more comprehensively than she could remember. She had simply been glad to have created a little more space in her storage area. He invited her to come over to his Cambridge Street Hall student room. His lair was to his liking thanks to her kindness, he said.

'The books have already been useful...it's not all on the internet you know!'

Of greater interest to Anju was the fact that Berin, whom she had always regarded as a somewhat spoilt individual, was now involved with volunteering, sometimes on a Saturday night of all nights, taking food and blankets to some of the homeless on the city streets. His mother had told her because she was worried about his safety. When she had a chance she wanted to know:

'Don't you miss going out with your mates on a Saturday night?'

'A bit, but it's not every Saturday night and Friday night's often our main night. You know, the party night!'

'How did you get involved? Who's running the show?'

'It's a guy called Father Tim, from Salford...they just put out an invite on social media. I think he's got something to do with a church, I don't really know. A mate of mine was doing it.'

Anju took up his offer of visiting a couple of days later, mainly out of curiosity about his life, especially the volunteering, and she was pleased to see that her offerings had made his room far more pleasing than her own had been in her varsity days.

'How is your help received? When you go volunteering I mean.'

'You mean do some see as it as patronising? Yea, it does feel a bit like that sometimes. Not usually though. Mostly they want what you are giving them. They don't care who is doling it out or why. A few are a bit scary...strung out, or numb looking.'

'I see.'

'There was this one guy, last time, a Bengali I'm sure, who shouted at me. Little guy, very loud and angry. First in Bangla, I think, then English.'

'No big brotherhood scene then! Did he try to talk to you in Bangla?'

'No. But let me tell you...it was ironic or something...but he had this birthmark, right here on his cheek which, well...it looks exactly like a map of the Indian sub-continent...!'

'Hang on. Just say that again!'

Whilst Berin more or less repeated what he had just said, Anju put her left hand up to her face, responding to his description.

'This must be the same chap I saw at my storage place...the man called Mr Choudrey who insisted he had an appointment with me at the Town Hall offices the other week about his homeless mate... looks like a tattoo doesn't it?'

'Right. Well, he was really mad with me. I copped for a lot of grief from him. He made out that it was entirely my fault that he was homeless and what use was soup when he needed a job and a roof over his head.'

*

'Berin you've got a visitor,' announced his mate when Berin arrived outside his room opposite the kitchen in his hall of residence. His mate had emerged from the communal kitchen to make this announcement. He looked both nonplussed and hesitant.

'He's in there, having beans on toast and tea. I don't know if I did right, but he said he knew you. He looked in a bad way. I knew you'd be back soon.'

'What do you mean? Who is it anyway?' Why he asked this before he peered round the kitchen door, he wasn't sure because he wasn't at all surprised to see Anju's Mr Choudrey eating furiously.

'What are you doing here?' was all he could think of saying, and quietly at that.

Mr Choudrey continued chewing for a few moments, then turned to reveal the familiar facial map, a reddish hue of Indian Ocean now lapped the shores of the birthmark. Berin was not sure whether this was due to embarassment, or more likely, the effort of eating quickly.

'Like you...I was a student here once you know, study, learn...'

Some resentment had overtaken the surprise Berin felt. 'What on earth... what could you possibly have been studying, Mr Choudrey?'

'Ah good, you know my name. Well in this country...much opportunity, I study the business studies. That is what I study, as you ask me.'

Berin had frowned. Mr Choudrey had continued.

'At The Manchester Professional Studies College on the Thomas Street. You know it? No... I study there two years. I study hard and have the certificates...from the MPSC of Thomas Street. But I do not get worthy job yet. I want work.'

'Look, I'm sorry to hear that...but what can I do about that. You need to see a...'

Mr Choudrey, stood up suddenly, his jacket pocket brushing up against baked beans in the process and shouted: 'No, no, no no! No I tell you! I need see no-one but you! You are the one to help me! Not council, the Jesus people, no the this or that do-good people or officials people. It's you...my big Bengali mate...you who must help me! Help me!!'

At this point he took something from his pocket with which he wiped his mouth and marched out.

*

'But Anju, how can he think he's my mate?'

Anju had done some digging. 'He's an overstayer now, my boss reckons, but with the right support could have found work and applied for a visa. Never easy of course or straightforward. It's a mess now and much more difficult.'

'But what exactly does he think we can do...you know, I wonder why he came... and has no family or friends here?'

'I dunno what we can do. I don't know whether after seeing me, in the lift at the storage place...well, it's possible he was just hanging about here, under the arches, you know where they tend to all meet up in the day...and saw me coming and going.'

'Yea...and he saw your ID badge. Saw you as another Bengali mate! Took a chance to meet a top, very important Government person!'

'I dunno, anyway...hey, he will have picked up that you are at the university...a great scholar!...will have top job very soon. He didn't let on when he came to see me at work, too shameful perhaps, but has become increasingly frustrated and is taking it out on you!'

Berin looked up into the corner of the student common room and then back at Anju.

'I don't know now what to think...it was easier to help him, in inverted commas, when he was just someone in the street...what do I do next time I see him?...I suppose it will depend...where and when I see him, but it shouldn't, should it?...I can't have him living with me here though can I?! He must be here illegally...perhaps that's why he doesn't want official help...what do I do?'

Anju did not address his specific question but started instead to think aloud.

'Why does he think we can help him...our sense of community...in the old days you helped the people you knew in your street...practical help not all talking and theory...and you gave a little spare money you had or food to support strikers or those laid off...or those who were too ill to work...you are right, we can't change the system overnight to help him. We could campaign against the cuts I suppose...I understand... it's like he has the village peasant mentality still...oh that sounds awful of me, I know...it's like my parents.'

'I'm out of my depth ...'

'We all are! I can't accommodate him either in my tiny flat and I've only just got rid of one guy...and that was bad enough cleaning and catering and running around after him and he was supposed to care for me! Our Mr Choudrey will just have to try and claim a visa and work permit...turn himself over to the mercy of officialdom.'

Sure enough, three weeks later, Berin on the soup run found himself face-to-face with that face, muffled up against the cold with the southern states of India obscured by, Berin was a little bit pleased to note, a very thick scarf.

'Look, I'm sorry, but this is the best I can do for you, Mr Choudrey.' He hesitated, thinking that maybe he should offer a meal once a week in the Halls of Residence kitchen, but instead he pressed on with his key message.

'You need to see Mike, that guy over there in the red coat, he can start looking at options of official help with you. Do you want me to send him over? Mr Choudrey?'

Mr Choudrey, reached out for the soup, spat on the ground and looked as far away as he could.

The Careless Fielder

'How's that?'

It's a glorious Sunday morning on the patio outside the male ward of the National Orthopaedic Hospital, Stanmore, Middlesex.

'Not out!' exclaimed a nurse, hoping not to spill a fullish bedpan as she sneaked around the back of the slips, a shortcut to the sluice room.

Dave Bains, the Troop Leader, umpiring, enjoyed her appeal and caught her smile though he realised that she had not been in any reasonable position to form an accurate leg before wicket decision. He was in charge of this venture, bringing in scouts once a week to support a game of cricket for patients: a chance for them to be reacquainted with fresh air, enjoy exercise and have a bit of fun. He declined to raise his finger.

He noticed that the bowler had made no enquiry and was already being pushed back in his wheelchair ready to resume his run-up for the fourth ball of the over. Surely he'd be the first to admit that the delivery of the high bouncing tennis ball would almost certainly have flown clean over the chair standing in as a wicket, even if the batsman had been able to remove his heavily plastered leg in time?

The next ball was belted over the low perimeter wall of the patio area, and began bopping along at a hell of a rate up the grassy bank. Dave gave himself discretion as to the awarding of runs, sensitively taking into account each batsman's individual condition. True, he lacked the patient's full set of medical notes, but this slog from a young beefy fellow, he felt, needed to reach the very top of the slope if he expected to be rewarded with a boundary. After all, he only had one arm in a sling.

A boy hobbled after the ball. This was the lad, Dave realised, who had been in tears last Sunday when he had tried to entice him into joining the indoor rounder's session. The lad had been in too much discomfort and tearful pain. He was a long way from his Yorkshire home. What was his ...oh yea, Ritchie.

Dave was impressed at how Ritchie used his stick at full stretch to take some sting out of the following shot and, being unsure of reaching down to pick up, had simply whacked the ball back to the bowler, who applauded. Ritchie had grinned.

Two scouts were acting as runners for the patients currently batting, and their exposed knobbly knees reminded Dave of pistons firing flat out on a downhill express train as they strained to achieve maximum runs for their drivers. It was so pleasant outside today that Dave started having ideas about obstacle races for the summer.

Drinks were taken after stumps were drawn, chairs taken back inside, and beds pushed back to their berths in the ward. Dave went over to chat with John. He'd got to know him well over the many months John had been in the ward.

'How are you? I thought it was you I heard laughing...when that ball hit Frank's drip!'

'Yea. That was quite funny. Gave Frank a laugh at least. Well, I'm same as, same as...you know. Same mangled legs. Same sarcastic git. You know me.'

'Don't be too hard on yourself John, you've had...'

'Sorry, I know, you mustn't mind me. Others can be sweet and sour but I'm... just sour. I am. I know I am.'

'Well, you've got good grounds for being bitter...they failed you big time... you kept telling them to get that guard on your machine mended or replaced...'

'I know, but...well look Dave...I've been a bit of a sod today and I don't feel too good about it.'

'How come?' What do you mean?'

'It's uh...well...it's about that lad Ritchie...you know the young 'un over there by the door.'

'Yea, ok. I know him. I'm so pleased to see him on the mend today, he...'.

'That's the point. He looks so happy now, don't he? I was mean to him, Dave. I unloaded all my bleeding misery onto him. Really piled it on. Went on and on I did. Had to tell him all my hard luck story, all the graphic details with my legs...like I'll never be able to walk. He's only about nine or ten. Hang on...wait, before you say anything...you've not heard the worst. I then had to go and tell him all about my brother and his motor neurone, didn't I. Well of course, I didn't! But I did. I banged on about it. I did...I don't know...'

'Ok. Well...'

'I dunno...it was...there was just somethin' about the lad recovering so quickly and looking so pleased with himself...and then I thought about him gettin' out of here and going back so soon...all sorted...to his fancy vicarage in luvly old York...all patched up with his happy vicar family. It just riled me...but what a so and so I am. Why take it out on him? Anyway, Ritchie, he just laps it all up and says he'll send me, get this...a pc when he gets home. I was being sarcastic...you know...send us a postcard why don't you...and he says...I will... and do I want one of the Minster!'

Dave wandered over for a brief word with Ritchie, who surprised him by saying that he would miss this place: what with the radio on all day...he had heard the new Beatles record, 'Can't Buy Me Love' loads of time now, and made new friends, and bumped into Stan, the African prince...you know the porter bloke who said he remembered him from before...when he had been in here for months when he was three, because Ritchie was exactly the same age as his son, even born in the same Coronation week.

'Isn't that amazing?' Ritchie exclaimed.

'What...that he says he's a tribal royal? A prince you say.'

'No. That he remembers me! But if he's a prince...how come he wears that horrible brown overall and does all the fetching and carrying...he shouldn't have to push people about in wheelchairs or heavy beds ...'

'Not your usual royal duties, I agree. I suppose he...well, it's complicated... he would have to take what work was available. Listen Ritchie, I wanted to ask you...I'm interested about schools. You do schoolwork...doesn't someone come in?'

'Not really, no. Well, we do...we do do a bit. A tall woman...after lunch that is...we usually get round that boy's bed over there and do some reading and sums and things, but it's hard to concentrate because he's got this big pin like a huge needle sticking right through his leg...you should see it... cause they're trying to stretch it or something. I don't mean to stare... but I can't help it, I keep looking.'

'And are you looking forward to going back to your school?'

'Yea I am. I'm hoping to be in the cricket team. I should be. That would be great. My Mum got our churchwarden to coach me and everything.'

Monday morning: David Bains was in his office planning his workload.

Maureen, the Unit Secretary, called through the half open door.

'Mr Bains, you asked me to bring in Tony. He's here now. Is this a good moment?'

'Oh, I suppose so...yes, yes, ask him to come in.'

Tony ambled in. They locked eyes. Bains averted his first. It was the stale look in the fifteen-year-old eyes that had him beaten, plus the sallow complexion, the scent of sweaty clothes and what his wife had assured him was undoubtedly a stiff whiff of testosterone. He knew how superficial this all was, but nevertheless it made him feel uncomfortable with the young man. Then there was the fact of having to go through the incident with him—why he'd asked to see him. That sounded so civilised. Needed to get to grips with him urgently to repair the awful damage he, Tony, had done.

Tony, as usual, wasn't exactly arrogant sitting there in front of him, but he looked rather defiant, and certainly world-weary. No sense of a race to be run. Let other fools run, he would rather sneak off for a fag. Bains had the distinct impression that every day was a battle from which Tony emerged hardened further. He'd faced unpleasant remarks and name-calling, even here in the Unit. When staff had talked to him about it, he had shrugged it off as if it was only to be expected. Had we as a Unit failed to fully pursue...find out all we could, do more? Baines had forgotten for the moment who was fostering him now...so many moves...how does he remember where to set off to at the end of the school day?

He urged Tony to sit down and noticed again how powerfully built he was becoming, with little room in the Head of Unit office to stretch out his legs, and he did like to spread out.

'I hear you scored plenty of runs on Saturday, Tony. Well done!'

'Yea. I smacked a good few.'

'And it's good that Wellington School let you join their second eleven. You agree? Gives you the chance to play. We can't at the Unit offer you any proper cricket competition of course?'

'Yea. And they need me. All them poncy kids with all their posh kit an' they can't even hit the ball ... like what I can... bloody hard.'

'Which brings me on to the incident which has upset them.'

'What now? What...what you mean? There's no pleasing some people. They'd 'ave lost without me!'

'Tony, that's as maybe...but this is a serious situation. The Deputy Head rang me. They say that when you were fielding...that you...you deliberately threw the ball at one of the opposition batsman. Not once, but twice. Could have caused him terrible head injuries. Very embarrassing for the school. They had to make a humble apology to Brampton School. Grovel, was how they put it.'

Tony stared ahead at some point just above his accuser's head who wondered for a second what he was focussing on exactly. Bains knew nothing behind that merited the slightest attention, unless you admired blank walls. He continued with the inquest:

'Once could have been an accident, was how they put it to me. But the second time...the fellow was clearly home and dry...standing in the crease after making the run...fortunately...Tony are you listening...Tony!...right...fortunately he saw your missile coming in, and ducked and again, fortunately, the umpire was not in the line of fire. What possessed you? What on earth got into you? What were you thinking?'

Tony lowered his poker-player eyes and looked fully at his interrogator but said nothing.

'Well, Tony, tell me...talk to me, please.'

The clock in the office could now be heard by both of them as twenty or thirty ticks went by. Then Tony stared into Bains's eyes.

'The sod kept looking down at me...right from when their coach arrived. All the time having a laugh at me with his mates. I didn't like him. I could hear him bad-mouthing me when I was batting. He was a lump of...like all 'em white kids...white staff.'

Tony talked. Taunting came often when he was out and about, he said. The comments, the looks, the threats. Even black kids when he was on the streets, round the precinct. Then Mr Bains remembered Tony's case-notes that came with him on arrival...describing him as belligerent and half-caste...what an awful label for anyone...must be a better one...anyway that might explain the black kids...half-what?...half a person, and what the hell did caste have to do with it? Back to practicalities.

The Head of the Unit expressed sympathy with Tony's situation. Then quickly tried to coax any glimmer of feeling of remorse or recognition of how the incident would be perceived by those who wanted his initiative to fail. Bains didn't like the term 'experiment' in this context, but it was an accurate description. It could be easily abandoned or halted by Wellington.

'Look Tony, I've managed to succeed in getting them to give you one more chance. It was incredibly hard work, so you've got to...'

Was he listening? Bains let him go after a few mumbles from Tony suggesting he wanted the cricket thing to continue. He decided to act as if Tony had played his part credibly and shook hands with him as if they had made a successful deal.

Maureen then brought in his mid-morning coffee, early. And two biscuits.

'What is to become of Tony? I do hope he doesn't simply end up like so many of the others...you know.' She whispered, 'In trouble. Inside.'

'No. let's hope not. Actually I've been thinking...I've decided to go and watch his next match. It's on Saturday at Wellington School. They are playing another really posh lot. I'll have to clear it with home. I was going to take Tom and Lucy out...that's the trouble with cricket, you don't when they'll be batting or fielding...which order...terribly time-consuming business. I could take the children though I think Jenny has something planned...anyway they're too young.'

'Are you sure? Family should come first.'

'Well, there's a break this Sunday from the Scouts in the Community.'

Monday afternoon. Bains made sure he bumped into Tony in the corridor.

'Oh by the way Tony, I've made some arrangements so I can come and watch your next game on Saturday.'

'I see...keeping an eye on me are you? Well...whatever you like. Doesn't bother me.'

There are few things we can ever be really sure about as the years slip by, and we try to recall exactly what took place in the dim and distant past. David Bains believed for years after, that despite what he was saying, a faint smile could be detected in Tony's eyes, for a fleeting moment.

In Transit

**'Here, have a listen to this...it sounds promising...it's set in a prison...
she's a good writer I've heard...yea ok Norman, I'll turn it up a notch.'**

Norman, a teaching assistant, watched Les Mappin, Head of Art, turn up
the tuner volume as the afternoon 'Play for Today' began. Les and Norman
blithely used their first names in front of pupils, or lads and lasses, as Les
insisted on calling them.

Footsteps were heard moving stereophonically across the Art room from
the huge speaker next to Les's bike to the one over by the storeroom. Followed
by clangs and creaking. Then a crisp voice narrated:

*'I was pressed into service on 'E' wing. I hadn't been before, but they were
short-staffed. It meant carefully unlocking about a dozen-floor-to-ceiling gates
and heavy steel doors and, of course, checking each one had been successfully
relocked whilst dodging along dank, narrow corridors which suddenly, for no
apparent reason, changed direction, sometimes dropping down a step or two
or ascending abruptly with sharp twists and turns. Eventually I managed to
emerge up and out into the daylight of 'F' wing landing.*

*I was surprised to find myself standing directly in front of a woman, an
inmate whose orange floppy hair swung to the rhythm of her floor mopping.
She paused, lent on the mop handle, and searched my eyes, clearly expecting
a surprised reaction. After all, this was a high security prison exclusively for
male offenders. He must be in transition...is that the right term, I tried to
remember?'*

As he listened to the drama, thoughts of Fred flapped up into Norman's
mind and fluttered around. Fred had been Les's great friend from his days at
Art college in London in the late 1930s. Les often talked about Fred with a mix-
ture of deep affection and regret. Fred had been very popular apparently, even
though, on a whim, he often attended college dressed as a woman. Nobody,
Les would emphasise, batted an eyelid, even when Fred went heavy with the
mascara and high with the heels. Or, according to Les, he might one morning
appear in voluminous blue overalls sporting bright red lipstick and hooped
earrings. On occasions, even go unshaven, but have a bright chiffon scarf
circling his neck, plimsolls sticking out at the foot of a loud pin-stripe suit.

Les had hung on to the many portraits Fred had painted and occasionally
showed them in class when he wanted to challenge what he regarded as the
obtuse ideas that adolescents had about gender identity. Norman took a more
measured view.

'In my opinion there's a lot of bluff and bluster when teenagers talk about
such matters, Les. Don't always take what they say at face value...it's mainly

for show you know...hides a lot of confusion they might have... and maybe tension.'

Norman thought attitudes were changing now, becoming more sensitive. It was Les, he implied, who was stuck in his view...what with all his highbrow talk of patriarchal something and indoctrination and ideological this and that. He did agree though with Les about rampant gender stereotyping.

Only this morning Les had been on one of his favourite rants:

'Don't let anyone limit you... ideas of beauty change all the time. Don't let anyone stop you from becoming what you want to be, don't be mindless consumers of conformity.'

These outbursts had become more frequent with the passing years. What had triggered this, Norman couldn't be sure. Les would mutter occasionally about 'boring bourgeois conformity...they're so damn complacent'. Norman on those occasions would feel obliged to reprimand him. 'She's only twelve, you know.' Or, 'He's only repeating what he hears at home all the time.' This only served to encourage Les to redouble his efforts to educate, or enlighten his charges, as he saw his duty, or was it his mission? Les had no wife, no partner, no children of his own and it had to be said, although Norman never did say it out loud, not much interest in most of the individuals he taught daily.

Norman found it interesting that Les never revealed to pupils what had happened to Fred. Apparently, Fred had found that whenever he stepped outside college he encountered embedded bigotry and, sometimes, downright hostility. The worst thing, the most difficult aspect he often told Les, was that it was not constant. Not always predictable. This made it even harder to cope with in some ways. Always anxious, either a little, or a lot of the time. Once he had graduated, he found it impossible to settle. His had been a sad demise, a downhill, freewheeling drift into hard drug addiction and, before too long, a fatal overdose. Les told Norman that he lived with the feeling that he had completely failed his lovely friend.

'I could...in fact I should... have kept in closer touch. Looked out for him. It's as if I knew his brakes were knackered and yet I let him ride off on his own. I was too busy...not just with my job, but with campaigning and meetings. Fred wasn't interested in any of that.'

Norman put thinking about Fred to one side and glanced up to see who needed support next. He noticed a couple of lasses and a lad were absorbed in listening to the play. Ever since he had begun working with Les, more than twenty years ago, there had often been music and the radio playing while work was being done. Les didn't expect everyone to give the play their full attention, but it was there for those who might need inspiration. Most of the time he played jazz or classical music to classes, although at some sessions he insisted on utter silence—it depended on what he considered most appropriate.

The present Head teacher, on assuming command had described this music while you work approach as 'subversive'.

'And what about the knock-on effect Les?...they'll expect Monteverdi with their maths, Phil Collins with physics...'

'Now that would be a mistake, I wouldn't want to inflict that on anyone.'

'You get my drift though, Les?'

'No, not really, Headmaster. Anyway, you can't argue with my results, can you?'

This was always, as everyone knew, his trump card and the end of any further discussion.

As far as Norman was concerned, any objectors to the musical accompaniment, and occasionally a parent might tentatively comment, were focusing on the wrong thing. It was the visual stimulation with which Les lit up lessons that was more likely to stir their middle-class souls out of their stupor. That was what the Head, some parents and quite a few of the staff, if they only knew, might have found more objectionable.

Les loved his slide projector and its ability to throw huge images on to the wall he kept as a blank screen at the front of the Art room. Here he could show a huge range of material: his own holiday snaps of Castro's Cuba, Russia and the slums of Italian cities or favelas of Brazil; images of Benin sculpture and crafts, the wonders of Timbuktu; Heartfield collages; documentary photos of the continuing Vietnam war; the events of Paris '68; Asian workers in the local hosiery factories, and the demos he had been on to support them. Not forgetting the stunning black and white photos he'd taken of his poor mother's arthritic hands.

His mother, ninety now, lived with Les in the bungalow he'd designed and mainly built himself. Norman lived a little further along the same road and used to offer Les a lift. The response never varied from:

'You won't ever catch me in one of those infernal, mobile, metal coffins Norman!'

Les cycled, walked or ran everywhere. He once hot-footed it to the airport as he insisted he could travel light and his contribution to school sport was to coach the cross-country team. For a sixty-year-old he was so much fitter than Norman, a decade younger, and in fact most of the staff. He often wore his running and cycling gear of t-shirt and shorts in the classroom, even in the chillier months. His only sign of ageing was spiky grey hair and thick lens glasses. He claimed to be self-sufficient in growing fruit and veg, and gave away any surplus. He always declined the offer of the wine Norman made from Les's gifts, as he was strictly teetotal.

When Norman drove up the hill past the Mappin home he was usually certain that he could still just about detect the traces of the massive CND symbol Les had painted on his roof in 1980. He had designed it with the letters END clearly displayed around it to show his support for European-wide Nuclear Disarmament. A photo appeared in the Loughborough Echo to accompany the report of outraged neighbours. Norman suspected that this striking image may have been supplied by Les himself. He boasted in class on many occasions that he had made the rooftop sign large enough to be visible to passengers on planes arriving and departing from Castle Donnington airport.

'The jet-set need to see a strong message of support going out to those brave protesters. I promised my mother I'd do it and I've carried out her request to the letter!' Norman guffawed. But what, he wondered, had become of the push for European nuclear disarmament? After the council planners ordered the removal of his protest, Les had vowed: 'I'm not finished with the END yet...I'll plant it out in bright flowers in the back garden...even larger!'

Norman had now worked his way around all the likely candidates for support as the radio play concluded. At the next meeting of this advanced level group Les, inspired by the play earlier in the week, and with Bowie as backdrop, now embarked on requiring the pupils to sketch each other in pairs and to draw out, in two distinct versions, one with so-called feminine and one with more masculine features.

'See if you can make her look more masculine in one, or him look more... you know, the other way round. You must have two distinctly different portraits of your partner!'

Towards the end of the session, he then asked them:

'How do we perceive people...haven't we a tendency to fall into fixed ways of looking but not seeing the whole potential of the person, so to speak... write a paragraph exploring this in relation to your portraits.' Norman noticed plenty of puzzled expressions and thought, I've got a right job on my hands here, especially as Les had disappeared for a few minutes into the storeroom. However, Norman was pleased to suspect that far more stimulation and discussion went on in Les's classes than anywhere else in the school.

Talk and discussion was one thing Norman definitely wanted to do with Les the following Monday morning break.

'Les, I went for a walk yesterday with Fran, you know she's determined to make me exercise more...anyway...I noticed a bunch of gypsies camped on that spare land near Masons...you might even be able to see them from the back of your place? Gypsies, tinkers...eh, I bet your neighbours and those up by Masons aren't too happy!'

'Yea you're right there. They've been camped there for nearly three weeks, I'd say. I'm surprised my charming neighbours, who are up in arms…you're right…well I'm amazed they haven't been badgering you to sign their petition. They want them shifted… right away… as if they are a pest control problem… but I believe the Travellers have some legal rights and can stay put.'

'How come?'

'Well, you see, the land used to be a regular stopping place for Travellers in bygone times…it's only in the 1930s that they appear to have stopped using it or they only stopped there very occasionally in the forties and fifties. My mother remembers, or she thinks that she remembers…anyway, no one's organised a welcome party, yet…though I've been over a few times.'

'You what?!'

'I hadn't planned it. I was running through Bluebell Wood when a couple of these chaps popped out from behind some bushes…'

'What…how do you mean…popped out? Were you frightened? Sounds scary.'

'No, no …it took me aback a moment…they were rooting around for fire-wood I think…and sprang up as I was passing…well I suppose it did startle me a bit, but they seemed to sense that and started talking in a friendly way. They invited me to their place, so to speak. They seemed to think I had expert knowledge… of the woods I mean… and the local scene.'

A few days later, having continued chatting about the unexpected visitors to the town, Les showed Norman a copy of a letter he had just received from the Head, from Charnwood Council. It said that following various meetings and liaisons there was now an agreement that the school offer access to a limited curriculum to a couple of young people from the temporary Travellers' camp. This represented part of the Council Diversity Initiative (CDI), an initiative…at this point Norman stopped reading, scratched his head and handed the letter back to Les.

'Can't they have home tuition, Les?'

'What…and how pray do I carry all the silkscreen kit or the kiln on my bike, Norman? Do you think we just lend them some pastels or paints? I am relying on you to support this initiative as they call it…you know what we'll be up against. Just don't put your head in the staffroom for a while…not that we hardly ever do…can't stand all the reactionary claptrap you're likely to hear.'

'Yea, of course…I'm with you.'

'Great…and I don't know that they'll want pottery or silkscreen, but I want to give them the chance.'

They were interrupted by pupils pressing on the door keen to resume work.

Over the next few weeks Les reported to the Deputy Head who responded in turn to education officials at the Council who kept asking for feedback on the progress of their pioneering initiative. One particular officer, Steve Wright, it was said, was wanting to make waves, declaring to colleagues that there was now growing support for CDI.

Les reported that Cathy and Sean from the Travellers' camp were showing a lot of interest in the art activities they were doing and had already demonstrated a fair amount of ability. He guardedly revealed to Norman that he was hoping to enter them for 'O' Level Art. He anticipated stiff opposition and likely derision from colleagues.

Two and a half months after the two young members of the Travelling community had started with School, Mr Mappin had formally approached the Deputy Head to seek his approval regarding the 'O' Level application. He sounded hopeful and said that he was minded to grant permission, but warned Les that the other two subject areas Cathy and Sean were attending were rather hit and miss at the moment. Cathy was responding quite well in English though.

One evening, shortly after seeing the Deputy Head, Les had dropped back into School from the Town Hall following a lively campaign meeting for more allotments. He wanted to sort out the contents of the kiln so that he could fire it up first thing in the morning. Having done this, he was just on the point of swinging his leg over his mount to cycle home when a rowdy group of staff and former pupils spilt out into his path. They parted to let the Head through who lurched rather in his rush to catch Les before he could ride off into the sunset.

'Hi Les, say why don't we ever see you at our reunions? You'd be most welcome you know. It's not just the Old Boys now of course, it's also the Old Girls now of course and that's more fun as they...well....I'd better stop there! anyway, what I want to know is why on earth you've backed those two Traveller kids to pass an 'O' Level...with the best will in the world Les they won't stick around...the clues in the name, you know.'

'I don't think they'll be evicted Headmaster, they seemed to have settled and one or two work at Bowen Marquees, for example. The council are taking a positive approach to the situation, making the best...'

'But it's simply not in their nature, not in their culture.'

'Things are changing and if they receive a warm welcome and some encouragement...some will settle you know.'

'I've heard that they are getting bullied. I know it shouldn't happen and we can say as often as we like that we won't tolerate it...but look here, it's all just one more headache we could frankly do without. We're not a charity after all, not a branch of social services, are we? I know you're full of good intentions, but really...be reasonable.'

'Well, Doug reckons…'

'Oh yes, Douglas, my good old Deputy Dog. You know I gather that his darling grandmother, or was it great granny, was in fact a tinker woman…roamed around that dreadful wild west bog land… in dear old Ireland…anyway, he's being a sentimental sod…Les, you must realise it's all just such a frightful gamble.'

'No, Headmaster, I've thought a lot about it. I've talked to their parents. They absolutely understand what's at stake, their responsibility. They deserve…'

'Huh, well, it's your reputation on the line with this one…let's be clear… on your head be it. Don't dare come whimpering to me when it all goes pear-shaped.'

Next morning the kiln was ready, the class assembled and eager, all systems go. However, there was no Cathy or Sean present. No sign, no word. This was unprecedented. A sickening blow Norman felt. He wondered if Les was feeling numb too.

The following day, the same thing happened, or didn't happen, and still no message. Friday was their last slot of the week in Art and when they failed again to appear without an explanation, Les told Norman that he would let the Deputy Head know and go and visit the camp that evening.

'I'll come with you if you like…if you think…?'

'I would like that, Norman. Cheers!'

Les reported back to Deputy Doug on the Monday morning with a depressing tale.

'Sean Quinn's Dad, called Michael, had been with this other Traveller just browsing the market in the town centre…this would be a few days ago now. They got really interested apparently in that big stall which flogs old tools. Do you know it? Anyway, Michael says he was simply examining a large clamp which would be useful as he often makes and repairs various items. He does have one but it's not very good, so he was keen to replace it.'

Les told Norman later that Doug kept glancing up at the clock in the room saying he was late for a meeting, but he had pressed on with the full details.

'So this clamp was one that the stallholder was selling and Michael picked it up to have a good look, as you do…suddenly the bloke started yelling at him to put it down, swearing at him, calling him all sort of disgusting things… according to Michael. He tried to explain that he was interested in buying it…meanwhile the burly assistant of the stallholder…and I know the chap he means…rushes round and starts wrestling the clamp off him and pushing him away. Michael says he froze, stood his ground, was shocked at what was happening. His friend came to his rescue and…Michael was honest about this…

they tried to shove the bloke back...meanwhile the stallholder came to put his oar in and so the four of them...well... found themselves engulfed in a fistfight.'

Doug seemed about to interrupt the tale, but Les had continued.

'As you know, the cop shop is practically on the doorstep at that part of the market and someone must have called them...'

'Any charges, charges for assault and affray or grievous bodily?' Doug had wanted to know.

'Well, there is one good reason to be hopeful. Two people have given witness statements to the police to confirm that Michael and his mate didn't initiate the scrap. I know one of them, Pete, and he told me all this.'

'That is fortunate...you mean someone's, or two folk I should say, are prepared to stick their neck out for a couple of gypsies?'

'Yea. I know Pete through Amnesty and he was on the hospice charity stall at the time...had a clear view of everything.'

'Whatever...anyway any chance of your absent students returning to the fold?'

'I think so. Michael says that Sean wants to carry on with art at least and has one or two friends now in that group.'

At their usual lunch break sitting outside at the back of the Art block, Norman and Les chewed over the pros and cons of the situation.

'Is it going to work Les? Will they stay the course, deliver the goods, or are you, I mean we, are we backing a lost cause?'

'I don't know, Norm. The Council could respond to all the objectors by simply turning them off the site...anyway, I'm going to do my damndest to see this through.'

'Yea. I reckon some folk are not above being sneaky and spreading litter around the site...then starting up ugly rumours about what goes on there!'

'I don't know about that. In fact, I just don't know. Must keep our expectations high, that's the main thing. After all, it's already been a relative success... shown a few people...we've all learnt a lot I suppose.'

'Oh yea, it's opened my eyes...as you know I was pretty sceptical. It's been hard on Cathy and Sean mind...they've had to be tough. Yea, it's been a good start.'

The return of the two truants later that week was a cause for celebration and a strong vote of confidence for Les.

'Although I have to say Norman, I still feel it's in the lap of the gods.'

'Well, when I walked past the other day...you know with this new fitness regime I'm on, I noticed that the camp looks well established, pretty orderly and even quite cosy. I think they're maybe dug in for a long stay.'

Spring advanced and the examination season stealthily moved towards them from over the horizon, gaining momentum daily. Catherine and Sean continued to apply themselves enthusiastically, even taking work home.

Then, however the worst happened. A fortnight before the first practical test the two Traveller teens were again absent. This time though there was a message. It came from Steve, the Education Department's Outreach Engagement Liaison Officer. Les was urgently called to the staffroom by a colleague to hear that Sean's father had bitterly complained about the content of recent Art lessons and the issue of exploring the theme of gender identification. No son of his apparently was…and here followed what Steve described as a long and angry diatribe of objections to what Mr Mappin was allegedly teaching. Steve would rather not go into details over the phone but agreed to meet with Les after school later that day.

'Les, having heard how distressed Mr Quinn is…and I know his views are abhorrent to us…leaving that to one side and wanting to get the initiative back on track, well, you will have to apologise and…'

'I've got absolutely nothing to apologise for!'

'In that case, I'd say, you've lost them then.'

'Look, I'm happy to talk it over with Mr Quinn. I have had to a few times, you know…talk to parents…had to the other week actually…I managed to calm them down. I always emphasise how impressed examiners are with originality, you know…independent critical thinking and expression and all that sort of thing…that usually works. Only wish it were true…about examiners I mean!'

The discussion went back and forth and roundabout for quite a while, but it was agreed that Les should enter the lions'den again. It was definitely worth a try. In fact, he made two visits over consecutive evenings. The first person he reported back to was Norman.

'It's no go with Sean I'm afraid. His Dad is adamant. He will continue with some basic English study…and…hey, cheer up Norman, you lose some, you win some…Cathy's fine with carrying on. Doing well with English too…but they should have put her in for an exam. Her mother is so pleased anyway and if she passes Art, and I think she will, it will be a right good qualification… might encourage her to carry on.'

'Oh right, ok…right, that's not a bad result I suppose…the Head will give us plenty of stick of course…make out that it's the worst thing to have happened to this fine institution in a thousand years of building a reputation for…but, hey…you're right, it's a pretty good result. A case of half-full, sort of.'

'Yes…yea, I'll drink to that…if you make it one of your non-alcoholic concoctions!'

Sanctuary

Once, a parishioner calling at the vast Victorian vicarage and grounds to discuss the arrangements for the baptism of her little darling, had been startled by the sight of the Reverend Rob Field stepping out suddenly from dense shrubbery, shrouded in smoke.

Kitted out in US Army surplus combat fatigues, the cleric was also sporting a black beret and sunglasses along with his dog collar. A plume of orange from a flamethrower scorched the ground ahead of him for a considerable distance. The visitor was alarmed, and she stalled and stared. Once the vicar of Osbaldwick had sensed her presence and the flame was flicked off, she regained her composure and approached him. The necessary arrangements for the sacrament were concluded in Field's study, once the hall, with children playing badminton, had been crossed.

Mrs Field—Sue—enjoyed telling this tale along with the anecdote of the time when her husband had used the flamethrower in the attic. One January day, Rob had decided this was the only solution to unfreeze their water tank. She was just reminding him how stupid and dangerous he had been when they were interrupted by shouts from two of their sons bursting in.

'Dad, Dad, I've just seen a black bloke coming up the drive, with Ben McCann!'

Sure enough a minute later Ben, an old friend of the Fields, led now by the boys, bounced in with a young chap close behind.

'Rob, this is Luther, a buddy of mine. Luth, I'd like you to meet Reverend Rob Field, a dear old pal, and his sidekick Sue. Ok Rob?'

They drifted down to the kitchen and were soon handling mugs of tea. Sue noticed that Luther hardly touched his.

'Sue, Rob, we need your help. Luther here needs somewhere to stay for a night or two...while he waits for the rest of his band to come over from the States. They're doing a tour of the UK you see. I know it's short notice and we've just landed in on you...but, look...is there any chance we could take advantage of your wonderful attic room for Luther here to crash...it's not...or is it already occupied?'

Students weren't due for at least a week, which Sue realised Ben probably knew. She glanced over at the short stocky figure of Luther, sporting a frizzy hairstyle she later learnt was called an afro. He smiled back sheepishly, leaving all the negotiating to Ben. His occasional comments turned out to be in an accent heard most often in Harlem.

Swiftly installed in the attic accommodation, Luther announced he would like to rest for a while, and he wasn't in need of anything.

'Thanks all the same Sue...Reverend.'

It was only when they were back in the kitchen, two floors down, that Sue and Rob talked through this development and agreed that the arrangements were very vague, but assured each other that it would all work out fine.

Early evening Ben rang from Leeds.

'Thanks again, by the way. I knew I could rely on you two.'

That evening, struggling up the back stairs with a pile of laundry, Sue heard an odd, strangled cry from around the corner of the corridor beyond the bedrooms, near the bathroom. When she reached the scene, at the foot of the attic stairs, Luther was disappearing back up through the beaded curtain to his lair. Rob's mother was standing stooped, in her dressing gown, mouth agape, pale and trembling slightly.

'Who on earth was that? A very black man I've never seen before just... well, he emerged from the bathroom and quite bumped into me. It gave me rather a shock I can tell you...I thought you said that you would let me know Sue...you know...take the trouble to introduce me to the new students...when they arrived.'

She tottered into the bathroom and locked the door firmly. Sue turned and having brushed aside the beads and her initial tentativeness, timidly mounted the attic stairs up to Luther. She knocked forcefully, reasoning that this was after all her home and wishing that Rob was doing this instead of her. He was out parish visiting. Why couldn't he do some visiting here, right now?

The attic door was swung open; Sue coughed, taken aback, by the smoky atmosphere.

'Oh, please, no smoking in there. We have an agreement with the university that there is to be absolutely no smoking and I know you're not a student but anyway...'

'Sorry, Mrs Reverend Sue.' Luther pinched out a large-looking, odd-looking cigarette.

'I'll not do it again. Sorry.'

'Well I am sorry...I didn't get a chance to tell you about Mrs Field senior... she's back living with us. I hope she didn't upset you or ...erm, say anything untoward?'

'Oh no, it was fine. She was...I hate to be rude...but look, I need to get more rest, urgently.'

Sue retreated and walked along to the other side of the house and received a fairly subdued response from Rob's mother.

'It was quite amusing I suppose. Don't worry dear, you know I've seen more coloured folk in my time than you...all those years in India. Though of course it's been a while. Lovely brown eyes by the way.'

As she left the old lady and made her way down the grand front stairs, Sue found herself stepping back to fond memories of Rob singing one of their old favourites, 'Lovely Brown Eyes'. By the foot of the stairs, and despite the sound of children creating a commotion, she paused for a moment to treasure her memories of youthful summer days, playing tennis, mixed doubles in an afternoon, before cycling off to daring dances in Carlow or Kilkenny in the evening. She smiled. Rob hated all that, especially any posh dances now, having to dress smartly. He always fiddled ineffectually with cufflinks and became exasperated, needing help.

Suddenly the shouting came right up to her. Her youngest was crowing: 'Mum, there's smoke coming out of the attic, at the front. I've seen it. That man up at the top window, up in the attic way above the front door.'

They sped out of the side-door and made their way past the outhouses and garage to the drive, where looking up above the front door they could see Luther's head poking out through the flung-open window. He seemed to be holding something precious. They watched as he bowed his head forward and cupping his hands inhaled with fervour. Almost devotional, Sue thought. Also, she reasoned, he wasn't actually smoking in the house, so she had better let him be at the moment. She would mention this to Rob though, the second he returned and see if he had any clear idea when Luther might be leaving.

Next morning, for elevenses, or in Luther's case, breakfast, Polly, the Help, was in the kitchen and Luther watched her as she made him a mug of coffee and some toast. She pulled out a chair for him and removed a cold and greasy piece of toast dropped earlier, wiped the seat and smiled at him.

By the time Sue was able to join Polly, she found them deep in conversation. She was disappointed when, as soon as she sat down, Luther announced that he must be off. Still, it was a chance to learn what Polly had been able to discover.

'It was fascinating. He told me all about what it's like where he lives. Just fancy Sue, New York, New York...although I know it's not all glamorous fancy apartment living. In fact he said it's pretty poor where he lives and people have no end of problems. He does go to church though. He loves gospel music. He only started going when he was passing by this church where he could hear wonderful music...drifting out. He said it was far out. He did tell me who it was and that everyone should...turn on to it man! He plays the saxophone... and is a big fan of Johnny someone doing Lovely Supreme...something like that...I can't quite...you know I couldn't help thinking of Angel Delight! Oh, it could be John Coldtrain. Some name like that, I dunno.'

When Luther's stay for a night or two had become a four-night residency at the vicarage and with no respite in sight, Sue felt that she had to be firm with Rob, consumed as he was with his crossword. It was now Friday with the first of their two female students due to arrive on Monday.

Ben was summoned.

On arrival Rob was absent so Ben chatted to Sue for a while about nothing in particular, but kept asking when Rob would be back. He then climbed up to the top of the house to talk to Luther.

Sue couldn't decide whether she felt relief or further frustration: relief because Ben was here, but frustration because he was still so vague about 'Luth's departure schedule'. All he had said was that their American visitor would be leaving as soon as possible, today if it could be arranged. Why had he come and why was he going, and going where? Why couldn't he bring her up to date on the arrival of the touring band?

At five-thirty-five the vicar returned, saw an unfamiliar car parked by the front door and then spotted Ben and Luther strolling around the grounds. So he joined them.

'Ah, Rob, glad you're back. Yea, I borrowed that car for the day from a mate. We're just inspecting the estate. Your vicarage, well I know it's not yours... reminds me so much of all the manses and vicarages in Ireland...you remember...usually grand yet shabby. Now, I need to know, has anyone been asking after Luther?'

'How do you mean?'

'Have you had anyone calling, enquiring about visitors at the vicarage? Anyone like the police, or anyone official or indeed any talk about our man here?'

'Now Ben, you are losing me. Anyone like the police? You mean have the police been knocking on our door and asking if we have Luther on our premises?'

'Yes, that's what I'm asking.'

'No...but Ben, why would they? Listen, there must be something going on here...that you've not told us.'

The three figures had stopped and stood facing each other.

'You are right Rob. We should come clean. Sorry. Luther is...well, he's on the run... from the U.S. military. He refuses to do another tour in Vietnam...I'm not talking music here, but as a G.I...I know, you'd think he would be safe here. We're not at war are we? But the police...the local police chiefs love to score brownie points by handing over anyone suspicious to the U.S. military police.'

'You mean...?'

'Yes. Good grief, in the blink of an eye, Luther could be in a military prison in Carolina...say, late tomorrow or early Sunday. Just think of that, Rob.'

'Well, now that's all very well...'

'You see they're looking to make examples. The war's not working out very well and they're trying to tighten up on draft dodging and deserters. I knew you and Sue would be sympathetic Rob, but I couldn't run the risk of coming clean with you – it wouldn't have been fair either. The less you know the better! Thing is I couldn't locate a safe place for him to move on to. I'll find somewhere soon I swear.'

'Yea, I'm real grateful Reverend Rob for what you done. Letting me stay with ya.'

'But why are you telling me now Ben?'

'Because we owe you and Sue an explanation and...we want you to know why you mustn't tell anyone. Careless talk...and all that.'

They moved under a chestnut tree and Rob said he would like to know more from Luther about his life.

'Well...I'm twenty-two. I'm in a jazz combo. I was conscripted jus' after I turn nineteen, jus' when my music was taking off. Then spent nine months in 'Nam. Complete nightmare, I tell ya. Man, you wouldn't believe what's going down, down there...no way. Yer buddies gettin' legs an' arms blown off front of ya screaming...chopper warships goin' in ahead an' layin' homes to waste, burnin', everythin' burnin', everythin' exploding...ever smelt flesh burnin'?'

'Er, I did hear... some sickening details in the paper. There was a news report...gruesome.'

'Yeh, well, lemme stop you right there padre...it ain't our war, see. It's got nothing to do with me an' my black bro's. Even them upright dudes in the Bronx churches an' all say that. It's why I came o'er to London. My brothers git me over here... no way I'm gonna fight Mr Whitey's war. Let them white suckers go, if they be so inclined. I heard me a preacher say once what hell is like and, well, that's pretty much 'Nam for ya.'

'So what you're saying is...'

'My bro's given me contact details here, you know like safe houses...but it all gets a bit hot, man. Keep thinking I being watched, so I hitched me to that Chelt'nam to find this here fine gentleman...I knows him when we toured couple of years back and, well, he gotten me papers an' thought it best I move up north.'

Rob looked at Luther and felt that a man was emerging from a shadow just before he was about to disappear, presumably never to be seen again.

'So, this business about waiting here for your combo members or group to meet up with you, is simply not true?'

'No—well, it's mainly true. They is over here. They's older an' won't be shaft...drafted. I wanna meet up with them, but it's too damn risky, so I can't.'

For a few minutes they continued to discuss the war and the draft. Ben wanted to be off.

'We must get Luther safe. Thank you Rob...please thank Sue from the bottom of our hearts for helping us. Rob, please...do not trust anyone asking anything...no matter how plausible they appear.'

'Sure. I'll tell Sue.'

Before retiring to bed Rob mulled over what Luther had said about not wanting to fight an unjust war, or a war in which he felt he should have no further part. Rob thought of his father, a conscientious objector in the Great War, the war to end all wars. He pulled open the filing cabinet and took out the diaries his father had faithfully kept describing the war years. Would he have understood Luther's anger at being considered expendable, too young to die...fighting Vietcong communism? After all, he, Luther, had few prospects apart from his music, back home? All Uncle Sam could offer him was a chance to murder or torture or be killed thousands of miles from home. When Rob had asked about the anti-war movement, Luther had simply replied sharply:

'Our voice ain't heard by nobody!'

As he turned over the tidy handwriting of the diaries, he found a lot of common ground between the young man from the Bronx and the Methodist Minister.

> *Had a debate with Davies as to whether it is possible to be in the army and still be a Christian...meanwhile the guns are shaking the place with their thunder.*
>
> *Our new surgeon, Lt Bell, got to work straight after dinner—his first case was one of the Norfolks, the fellow was struck above the forehead and a piece about the size of a penny was gone. A portion of the man's brain was protruding; it looks as if he can't hold out long. The other case was a poor chap who was struck by a shell, and had four wounds; both feet, right thigh and left waist. Mr Bell and Mr Pirton amputated his left-hand, about one and a half inches above the wrist. After tea word came that 25 stretcher cases are coming. May peace soon come to our war-cursed earth!*

Luther hadn't mentioned peace once, it struck Rob. He had just said that the yellow brothers should be left to sort out their own problems their own way. If anybody who matters was bothered to find his opinion. Rob hadn't liked to be all Church of England, BBC-neutral and talk about superpowers and proxy wars. He read on.

> *When the convoy arrived at 10pm there were 18 cases, including one officer. Two were nearly dead and most were seriously wounded. One*

had an eye removed; two had injuries of the skull and brain necessitating trepanning; there were broken legs and arms; ruptured veins; wounds, bruises and putrefying sores.

Yes, Rob was glad he hadn't burbled on about taking a balanced approach, merits on both sides of the argument and all that.

Sister called me over to stay with a dying man; he didn't keep me long, about two minutes. We carried his corpse to the mortuary.

After tea an operation on a very nice chap, Guthrie; he was wounded in three or four places, but especially in the abdomen. On opening him it was found that the wound was fatal so the operation suddenly ceased and we carried him back to die in bed.

From what he knew and millions since had learnt, to die in a trench in that particular conflict was a relative luxury. Rob also knew that his father had been no coward. He had been mentioned in dispatches and issued with a medal for bravery, for going into no-man's land to try and rescue a wounded man, or at least recover his body. He turned to the relevant entry in the notebook giving the daily ordeals of Sgt RH Field RAMC.

There were two dead men in the trench as we went along and just as we got to the end a shell burst close by, the force of the explosion forcing me down. Coming back a bullet struck a noticeboard just as I passed it. Soon afterwards I think we heard of a man wounded up the line...when we got near, the trenches were battered about a lot and almost deserted. We found our patient in a sap leading to the German lines. There were three bodies, two on the wire...coming back we lost two of our number in the numerous bends of the trenches.

We attended one thousand one hundred wounded, and I worked all night. The next morning was Sunday, but except that darkness changed to light there was no other change and the guns, and the flashes, the wounded, the dead, the prisoners, everything was the same. I felt absolutely sick at heart to think that the nations have nothing better to do than to organise this murder. I thought of it all as much as I dared; here in front of us was war's harvest, and a terrible reaping it was. It doesn't do to let the mind dwell on this, or we might be inclined to desert.

Rob went on to read the passages describing mustard gas attacks, his father shocked by the delirium and delusions caused. He thought of the TV footage that kept appearing on the news of massive planes high above the jungles of Vietnam spraying Agent Orange. Defoliation, death, and now deformed babies. In 1917 the colour of death and utter misery was yellow. It had been blue before orange apparently in the early part of this decade. Monsanto, or was it Dow Chemicals, had changed their colour scheme recently. Not wishing to paint the towns red or the jungle blue... No hiding place for soldiers and now no escape for civilians. Yes, he was convinced his old man would have listened with concern and sympathy to Luther.

On Sunday, the church of St Thomas, Osbaldwick and Murton was well attended considering it was evensong. The congregation joined the vicar in saying: 'Almighty God, to whom all hearts are open, all desires known, and from whom no secrets are hidden...'

Before continuing he glanced up to view those present, 'here present' as the next prayer put it, and noticed Ben and Luther amongst the congregation. He always liked to emphasise that at St Thomas's all are most welcome, but still, this was pushing it somewhat.

His sermon was remembered afterwards by Ben for the sweep of cultural and topical references, including Rothko, Sharpeville, A Winter's Tale, and the ambitious way in which they were used to illustrate today's gospel. The preacher's father-in-law, whom Ben had met once, was given a surprise mention. Over from Ireland on a visit, he had been taken apparently to a performance of Waiting for Godot and had been intrigued even though Ben recalled the old gag that in the play nothing happens...twice.

As was customary, at the conclusion of the service Reverend Field hung about near the exit to exchange pleasantries with his flock before they left. When Ben and Luther arrived close enough to see the fine embroidery on Rob's stole they vigorously shook hands and urged:

'We need a quiet word...we'll just wait for you to finish up.'

Ten minutes later, in the deserted church they spoke in hushed tones:

'Listen Rob. It's like this. There was so much not right with the new arrangements. Sorry, but we need your help again...you see...well, we're trapped and they are closing in. The only way out is for Luther here to seek... let's call it asylum...or sanctuary, or whatever you want to call it...with you, right here in this church. I know it's a lot to ask, but for God's sake...sorry... anyway you've got to help us please. Will you?'

While the vicar was making sense of what he was hearing and starting to think through the significance, Luther chipped in: 'Don't worry 'bout nothin' Reverend Rob. We seen you got a bathroom...I mean toilet an' wash basin, in the vestry. I notice there's a kettle and all that. We be fine, don't you worry none.'

'But er...well uh, where will you...sleep, I mean...you know it's not warm, not summer any longer really...? Rob suddenly realised he was being swept along in their scheme.

'Listen Rob, we've got our sleeping bags. The pews will do fine and...if we take the liberty of using these lovely hassocks for pillows...we'll be well away. Don't worry. We'll keep well out of your way. We won't bob up in the middle of morning prayer in our undies!'

Rob sat down heavily next to Luther and said they could stay on tonight. He'd talk more tomorrow when he came to say his morning office at 7.45.

He didn't know quite what else to say, but blurted out: 'You've taken me by surprise, to put it mildly. You know you'd be more than welcome to come back with me and stay at the vicarage.' He tried not to imagine how this scene would play out at home if they did take him up on his offer.

'That's awful kind of you Reverend, but this is for the best, ain't it Ben?'

'The church as a sanctuary...Rob.'

Once out of his surplice and cassock and after he had talked through the locking-up arrangements with the new custodians, the sheer strangeness of the situation struck him. Post-evensong was usually a winding down moment in his weekly timetable. Instead, he found himself thinking all the way walking home: have I done the right thing; what on earth happens next?

Back at the vicarage, Sue noticed he looked strained.

'What's up, dear? A different, more difficult crowd in tonight? Any awkward customers?'

'Well, there were a couple of worshippers who...I mean...Ben and Luther for one, or two rather...'

'What! You're joking? Oh, I see, you're not. They've not come back here then with you for a night-cap or game of snooker?'

'No.'

'They've gone off then?'

'No.'

'They've gone back to Leeds.' Responding to a headshake. 'They're staying with friends in...'

'No. No!'

'Rob, what are you saying...or not saying?'

'It's complicated. No, what I'm saying is...it's simple, I suppose. Luther and Ben are camping out at church...'

'Camping?!'

'Yes, camping. Luther, you see, has applied for sanctuary.'

'Sanctuary?!'

'Yes, you know, the ancient right of sanctuary. I must just go and check if I've got any useful information...on the legal situation you understand... I think there's a time limit...twenty-eight days or something like that...we didn't exactly spend much time covering the subject when I was training... don't look so worried Sue, they're quite safe!'

After some time spent reflecting on the situation, especially after the children were all in bed, Sue wasn't thinking at all about their safety, but rather the moral issues and her husband's responsibility. At half-eleven, with Rob restless in bed she was moved to say:

'Here's a stranger, Luther I mean...and he's asking for the support of the church over a matter of conscience. I know it's awkward...inconvenient even... an intrusion you might feel, into our comfortable routine...but isn't this precisely the sort of issue we should be fully involved with. Our church...?'

'Yes, I agree and for Luther it's...'

'A matter of life and death! Kill or be killed!'

'Most of our congregation may actually have to now think seriously about it. I mean it will bring it home to them...this war and conflict.'

After a night of fitful sleep, Rob plodded down to church shortly after half-seven to say the Office of Morning Prayer. He carried with him a couple of sandwiches Sue had prepared for the sanctuary dwellers. Should he knock on the door? The whole situation felt strange, unsettling. He simply turned the handle and strolled in. They appeared to be in good spirits and reasonably warm for mid-September with no heating on.

'You're not the first. Your cleaner called. Gave us a shock hearing the door opening about 7.30! She said she usually cleans on Tuesdays but her sister from Chester is arriving shortly...this morning and she wanted an early start... anyway she scarpered.'

'Right, I see...this does mean though that word will be out, and soon, and all over the parish. She's not exactly the soul of discretion. Oh well.'

By mid-afternoon there had been two phone calls to the vicarage based on the cleaner's discovery. One was from the secretary of the Parochial Church Council who sounded incredulous. Said he didn't know what to say. Rob spent a fair amount of the afternoon ringing round friends and one or two colleagues to sound them out.

'It's a smart move by this Luther fellow—it's both a protest and a way of protecting himself.'

'The novelty will soon fade...they're having a laugh. They've taken advantage of you and your kindness, Rob.'

'It will show which side we, the Church, are on.'

Some raised practical points: How were his superiors going to react? What were they likely to do? Hadn't he better think about issuing a press statement or talk to the Diocese about one? One colleague suspected that the archbishop would be having his people searching for an obscure ecclesiastical rule which would result in Luther's eviction.

On Tuesday, the Field boys returned from the shops to say everyone was talking about it. A PCC member had taken in some reading material, chocolate and fruit and told Rob it was a pleasant change from hospital and sick visiting.

Wednesday afternoon, Sue reported back to Rob the delightful news, she felt, that Kate had offered to do any clothes washing they wanted doing. She'd been into church to have a chat and reported that one of them, Ben, was about to leave.

Ben called at the vicarage early evening and told Sue that he would return as soon as he could, in a day or two.

Thursday was the rest day for the vicar. He went out for a lengthy walk as he was supposed to be in training for a sponsored Lyke Wake Walk. On his return, heading up the vicarage drive, a car turned in after him and parked up close, almost cutting off his access to his front door. Two men emerged and stood there a moment, then introduced themselves as detectives.

'It's about your new lodger, Reverend...you know...the one down at church.'

'I've nothing I want to say...nothing I can tell you beyond what you probably already know.'

'Hang on a minute, you can't just wander off sir...after all, he's in your church and we want to know...'

'It's not my church, it belongs to us all, the whole community. Open to anyone...and they can stay as long...'

'Now you're being perverse, or at least evasive, sir.'

'Look if you want to speak to him...'

'We just call in down at St Thomas's, it's open to all...is what you're going to say?'

'That's right. So what do you want from me? What exactly?'

'We think that our best chance of him coming with us to the station, to explain his absconding, is if you can persuade him that it's in his best interest...'

'I'll stop you right there. I don't think it's in anyone's best interest...well except the US military who simply want to prevent an epidemic of this type

of action. They probably want to make an example of him, his legitimate protest. You'll have to drag him out forcefully if you can't persuade him...and that
would desecrate the sanctuary of our church. Wait let me finish! The Press,
you know, are very interested in this story...you'll have read his statement in
yesterday's paper...the *Evening Press?*'

No answer as they had already turned towards their vehicle before the
vicar had finished speaking, slamming their doors and shooting off.

After they left, Sue went off to fetch a letter, delivered by hand that morning. Addressed to *The Incumbent*, it informed him that *the presence of this
deserter in our Church is a disgrace and having spoken to several other members of the congregation, we will not be attending church again until the
offender has been removed.'*

'It's Bill Cooper complaining about Luther. Don't suppose he's willing to
sit down and talk to Luther. Oh, and he's sent a copy to every senior member
of the Church of England he can think of.'

Sue had more positive news. 'A few students came down here from Hes-
lington to offer their support and did go off to talk to Luther. They said they
will start a university support group or something...'

She continued: 'We should have a meeting to plan our next moves?'

'Yes, we need to be prepared. I just think the American authorities will
not want to let sleeping sanctuary seekers lie. They will want to nip this in
the bud...before hundreds of others arrive! It's already starting to happen in
Canada apparently...very much on the quiet of course.'

Next day there was a surprise call from Bishopthorpe Palace. The archbishop wanted to meet Luther that afternoon. He arrived with the area dean
but insisted on going down to church on his own to talk with Luther.

Clearly Luther had impressed him. He began by directly quoting Luther:

'No Vietnamese ever called me a nigger. Excuse my colourful language...
but that's how he put it. Why am I fighting these bro's? They bin having their
struggles too man...just like my people.'

These statements and rhetoric sounded almost amusing in his eminence's
stilted Queen's English tones.

'Sounds like Cassius Clay or that Malcolm X to me,' Rob suggested.

'Who...what...Well anyway, he's a thoughtful young man. Sincere I believe
...and spoke with a surprising depth of knowledge...about the shocking effect
that the bombing and fighting has had on villages and communities in the
areas he was in...perhaps I shouldn't be surprised he knows so much...after
all he's been there in the thick of it! The interrogation techniques the Americans are using...well, they are just stomach-wrenching...and as for that Agent
Orange...He looks so young...they're sending boys really, I think. On both

sides he says…you know the ones they capture.'

'Yes, he always talks about our boys…the brothers…'

'I know—the black guys in the US Marine Corps. Don't misunderstand me Field, I'm not anti this war or pro…I'm not keen on atheistic communists in South East Asia or anywhere else come to that, but the Americans are unjustified…in how they're conducting this war…well, playing into their hands…have lost their moral compass completely…'

'So what about our role…'

'Whatever people think about the superpowers, proxy wars and all that, what's come through to me…well, I have to say…I agree with your reported remarks in the Press. What we have here is an individual who welcomes the sanctuary we are able to provide.' He looked directly at Rob.

'I agree. We provide a safe space and time to reflect or shelter. I think a lot of our congregation are quite bewildered by it all, but that's not a bad thing… even if it does divide opinion…makes things awkward for us.'

'Yes. It may be difficult to keep all on board and not upset some. I don't know what will happen next, but there must only be passive resistance on Luther's part and by any of his supporters. Understood? Look, let's pray.'

What happened next may or may not have anything to do with any prayers.

'What? Did you say…police? Ok…and you're on your way now? Speak up you're faint…I am shouting, it's a bad line! …Have I heard you right? You want me to accompany you on this raid to break the sanctuary?…You want me to get Luther out…and do what? Hand him over to the US mil…Is there really no alternative…? What, say that again…you'll be here in a few minutes…I have to wait here…until…'

Ritchie and his younger brother George heard their Dad's part of this conversation all too clearly. They had been about to set off on their bikes and were just checking for post by the front door, particularly seeing if Charles Buchan's Football Monthly had arrived yet. They listened a moment longer.

'What happens if Luther doesn't want to come quietly?' Their Dad was still shouting.

Ritchie signalled George to come outside with him and to be quiet.

'We've got to get down to tell Luther. Come on!'

They grabbed their bikes which had been abandoned where anyone could fall over them outside the front door. Ritchie pulled up his mount, jumped on and pedalled off hard. He was pleased to find that his brother could keep up. Walking would have taken them six or seven minutes but by bike they were up to the church porch in well under two minutes.

They charged into the church. It was empty. Shouting for Luther, they were relieved to see him creep out from the vestry holding a razor with foam all over his face. He had to insist that they slow down and only one of them speak at a time. Once he understood the main message, he shoved a few things into his rucksack and followed them out, wiping his face with the back of his sleeve.

'Take one of those old brollies, I think it's starting to rain,' shouted Ritchie over his shoulder. George pointed to the stack of left-behind umbrellas inside by the porch door.

Ritchie had been hatching a plan whilst pedalling down from the vicarage.

When Luther asked: 'Where you guys taking me?', Ritchie explained that they were going round the back way, taking the loop along by the old village green which would bring them back round to Osbaldwick Lane.

'It's a sort of back way, Luther. See we can wait up by the main road until we see 'em go past...the cops on their way down to church. Just you watch. Now... come on, we've got to hurry!'

In a minute they had skirted round along the edge of the tiny green, another minute and they had gone past the church hall and were up waiting to re-join Osbaldwick Lane. Luther stood alongside them, out of breath and anxiously peering through the bushes screening them from the police car. It should fly past soon. They didn't have more than a minute or so to wait.

'There it goes!', shouted George.

'What, how do you mean?', Luther sounded sceptical but Ritchie too had seen the police patrol car flash past with three men inside. Also he glimpsed his dad, there in the back.

'That was them...the cops...after you...come on!'

This was their green light to get going and they turned right onto Osbaldwick Lane. They knew it wouldn't take long for Luther's absence to be discovered.

'We've got to hurry. We've got to get past the vicarage and get off this road. Luther laughed despite his lack of breath.

'You guys watch too many cowboy films! Slow down...I haven't had much exercise recently...and this air sure is heavy.'

A hundred yards to the vicarage. The trio hurried by as it started to drizzle. Another hundred yards and Ritchie suddenly turned right into the council estate. He knew a shortcut to Tang Hall Lane and buses. Luther was pleased to see a slight slope downhill, but it was leading to the end of the road. George bringing up the rear, told him they had to cross the railway line.

'How do you know this track, pardner?'

'It's the way we ride to the library. Don't worry they say there are no trains and we've never seen one.'

'Definitely no Apaches!', added Ritchie.

A couple of minutes later Tang Hall Avenue was in sight.

Ritchie asked Luther: 'Have you got any money? You see, you can get a bus here and escape?!'

'I've gotten a few of 'em pound notes...Ben gave me.'

'Yea, but you'd better have this shilling and these pennies, six I think. They don't like to give change...I mean from notes, on the bus. Take it. It's our pocket money. Don't worry...just take it, please...we've got plenty of sweets and chewies.'

'You guys are too much. You my buddies for life. I hope all this don't land you in no trouble.'

'Ok. Look Luther...there are lots of people at that bus stop...

'A bus must be coming very soon...right?'

'Yea. But listen...get off at the bus station. Don't go to Leeds, Luth. That's where they are bound to look first. Anywhere else, get out of York.'

'That's right. An' I'll use the brolly a lot...keep it low...as the only black guy in town!'

'Oh great, here it is. Quick, get over there,' he yelled at the back of Luther's rucksack as the Marine on the run half-ran across the road.

The boys watched him take his turn, step up smartly onto the bus which would take him to the city centre. Who knows where he might go after that. Slowly they made their way back to the vicarage, but decided to give it a wide berth for an hour or so. However, after a few minutes or so, rain which had begun quietly as they left Luther became far noisier.

'This should help Luther if he keeps the umbrella low when he can. You know I saw it on the tele. '

When they reached the vicarage, they found out that there had been a search of the church, the graveyard and enquiries by the police in houses near church. No sign, no clues emerged, they had drawn a blank, the suspect had evaded their clutches. They tried to hide their annoyance and frustration. The police had had to tread carefully as the only person who knew of the sanctuary busting operation raid was the Reverend Field. Dad was telling their Mum how the conversation had gone. He enjoyed hamming up the part of Detective Inspector Stevens:

'Sir, I am asking you to give us a categorical assurance that you did not in any way tip off the suspect, this Luther character, did not give him to understand what was about to take place. To be absolutely clear, we need to establish that you did not phone him or contact someone who could reach the church prior to our arrival?'

'Are you alleging that I somehow went behind your back and am not to be trusted after you distinctly told me to maintain the strictest confidentiality? You rang to check my whereabouts, before then arriving at the vicarage five or so minutes later. There's no phone at church, so no means to contact Luther except by carrier pigeon. I spoke to no one apart from my wife...who would need to know about your imminent arrival and my unexpected departure.'

Though inhibited, the officer pressed on:

"Well, how did he know to leave this morning? You say he was there last night. That's what I don't understand.'

'No. I mean, yes, I agree with you, it is remarkable. Perhaps he could see the end approaching and didn't want to leave it to the last minute...but I am simply guessing.'

'Any idea, Reverend, where he might go? Is there anyone who might be tempted to offer him shelter and comfort, has anyone from the parish got pally with him?'

Rob said he had resisted telling them anything. He didn't let on that actually he was pleased that quite a few of his congregation had shown a caring Christian compassion. Or that others thought it was all a disgrace.

'I probed a bit, and said, "I half imagined that the Americans would have attempted to snoop on the situation...or even send in a couple of heavies."

'I think they felt that they were too late, once the case hit the Press and TV ...they don't want to add to the publicity...they like to work on the quiet and you see we're too far from any of their bases here.'

'I even asked: 'What about our secret service?"

'No comment, sir. I'm sure they will be working with...well, I'd better not say.'

As Ritchie and George heard all this sensational news about Luther escaping from the police raid, they looked uneasy and were rather quiet, Sue thought. She said nothing but did wonder if they knew anything.

She told Rob that Bill Cooper the letter writer had rung. He had simply wanted an assurance that the Field boys were safe and sound. He was worried about them. He had been out tidying up his garage and had seen them rushing past on their bikes being chased by that wretched asylum-seeker fellow. He hoped that they had got home safely. His first thought had been to phone the police...glad to hear that the sanctuary business was over. Wasn't it?

Half an hour later, Sue told Rob of the confession made by their sons of their morning's work. They both felt momentarily buoyed up with pride. How well their boys had responded.

Then pinpricks of anxiety were felt. Suppose there had been other witnesses, other reports to the police. He continued to feel deflated, so they talked about their guilt. Rob also said he felt more than a stab of remorse for having being swept along with the police raid.

'Technically, if we don't report in what we know, we are guilty of aiding and abetting a criminal activity or at least colluding.'

'But Luther wasn't breaking our law.'

'But that's not how our allies the Americans see it.'

'Well, our government is not supporting them over Vietnam, well not sending troops anyway and many in the Labour Party and even some Tories...'

'Say we shouldn't co-operate with the Americans over their military matters.'

'By the way...Polly knows about the great escape. Her friend Linda was just coming out of the newsagents opposite the church and saw them all flying out. Don't worry Rob, she says they acted out of kindness and she liked Luther, remember.'

'Yes, it was instinctive for them to want to help Luther.'

'Did you have any instructions from the Archbish or anyone...'

'No. Not since his visit. I was on my own. You know I'm actually grateful to Ritchie and George.'

'Why?'

'They make me feel better about my part in this episode. I know...I could always say I was intending to negotiate when we got down there this morning with the police...or at least I would have stopped them laying hands on Luther. But perhaps I'm kidding myself. When it came to the crunch...'

The phone rang—one of the churchwardens. Sue heard Rob's responses:

'But we don't know where he is! We have no idea if he'll get away with it, as you put it.'

'You mean if we knew would we tell? ...probably not.'

'Certainly not,' Sue added under her breath.

The headline in The Yorkshire Evening Press the following day proclaimed: 'Sanctuary seeker flees church!' There was a sub-heading, 'US Marine on the run again.' The local TV news showed shots of an empty church and ran a very brief interview with the incumbent who looked perplexed though talked about how pleased he had been with the role some of his congregation had played.

Reflecting over the following few days on how it had all worked out, Rob convinced himself that he would not have let them simply take Luther away. He couldn't have faced up to all those who had fed, washed clothes for Ben and Luther, or in many different ways had shown their support.

Ruminating a month later on what he had learnt from the episode, his thinking was interrupted by a shout from Sue. When she burst in clutching a postcard and he heard who the sender was, he joined in with her delight.

A message from Luther. Now in Sweden. It was addressed to all the Fields.

'Hey guys thanx for ever. Walked 4 miles outta York in the rain to Thursk Road. Took bus to Thursk an later Midb. Gotta boat from Tineside to Holland. Met Bros there. They helps me headup here which is cool. Sweden great man! Luth x'

When Rob rang Ben with this great news, he already knew. He still warned them about discretion and pointed out why Luther wasn't very forthcoming. Also he wanted to know if Rob and the church would support other sanctuary seekers on their way to finding safe countries.

All that Rob could think to tell him was: 'We'll have to think about that.'

A Reggae Song at Christmas Time

The presentation of the winter veg curry with its abundance of beet-root made the priest smile. He admired the topping of coriander cuttings. Glancing up from the dish caused his smile to widen further as his eyes beheld the wonder of the orange, burgundy and lime-green walls of the cafe. A Caribbean welcome in murky, late November, Salford. It had stopped raining as he had slipped out from the cathedral, a few minutes before, in search of a bite to eat away from the sacred spaces and the stuffy office.

Here he was with a new start in the North, far from his Home Counties seminary, looking to lend a hand where he could and expecting, before too long, to be a leader and guide.

After the meal, his body glowing and mind refreshed, he went over to thank the proprietor who said he was most welcome and to call him George. George was a man of gentle manner, all warm milk with a honey voice strongly hinting of a past life lived far from these shores. The backing of insistent reggae rhythms, accentuating the offbeat, had certainly made a shift of scene for Tim.

He promised George that he would be back soon. Though reluctant to leave, he set off with a spring in his step, but paused by the old Town Hall in Bexley Square, with its blue plaque, scene of the notorious riot of 1931 when unemployed men, their benefits decimated, had been bludgeoned by brutal police for wanting to be represented at a meeting inside the Hall. Brooding on this, he noticed now the drizzle thickening as he trod more slowly along Victor Street.

It became a daily ritual, for Tim to drop into George's cafe for lunch. He couldn't resist the hospitable attention of George's assistants. Motherly women, who insisted on bringing his order to his table every time.

'Oh, sure it's no problem, as the young say these days, Father.'

Most of the clientele were young, students he assumed judging from the overheard conversations, the books and files they carried, and included a few chaps from a sound production engineering school next door. Tim had no idea what that involved but the young man who told him was enthusiastic. There were not many women at lunchtimes, but one day he had noticed a small group of Young Mums and Toddlers, as his parish newsletter would have described them. They then continued to come on a regular basis, once a week on a Wednesday.

Nearly a month later, arriving for his usual lunchbreak, he found that on this occasion the cafe was packed, with only one place left, alongside the frail gentleman who appeared to be a permanent fixture. Oddly enough, George himself always served this elderly man and Tim wondered if he were in fact an old friend or family member. Certainly, no money ever appeared to change hands. However, any dealings between the two were brief and this seemed to rule out the possibility of kinship—or was Tim being naïve when it came to understanding the dynamics of family relations, as some of his friends sometimes said?

Tim did his best to engage the man at his elbow but only managed to raise the odd grunt and occasional scowl. He went out of his way through the following few days to sit next to this uncommunicative fellow with his haggard face and his limbs lost in his shabby coat, hoping to hear him say something. At the counter ordering a coffee, after a particularly lovely meal, but one bereft of any conversation, one of the women assistants quietly told him about Lee.

'He comes in around eleven thirty every day and stays 'til about two. He lives all on his own, lonesome, poor soul...hardly a penny to his name. Never looks like he'll last the long winter. We think he's an old friend of George's Dad...comes from the same village, in Antigua I think it is. Any road that's what I was told.'

This gave Tim plenty to mull over as he ambled back to the cathedral.

One thing he decided to do was to continue to make a point of sitting next to Lee after asking him if he didn't mind and taking no reply as permission. Day by day, he managed to gradually increase the grunt count and also noticed that there were signs of changes in breathing coming from Lee with some sharp intakes occasionally, and, most welcome, the beginnings of eye contact.

A few days before Christmas, a brazen bearded hipster, a term that Tim had recently been introduced to, came over, sat down, said he was called 'Tony' and asked Lee if he would help him with some research he was doing for his course. Did he like reggae or prefer ska, or bluebeat or some other genres that Tim didn't catch? Lee remained unable or unwilling to respond or express a view at all.

Tony then tried: 'Well do you like this UB 40 that's playing, 'Red, Red Wine'...great isn't it?'

Lee turned and stared at him, spluttered, looked very angry and then abruptly shouted out: 'It's an abomination! An a-bom-i-na-tion. Do you hear!'

Tim was pleased to hear this speech, but was unsure how to encourage Lee to add to this curt comment. George came over at speed.

'Hey, what's the matter? What on earth's going on?'

Surprising everyone, including George judging by his startled expression, Lee provided a very brief justification for his strong preference for the original Tony Tribe version of 'Red, Red Wine'. George readily agreed and a semblance of a discussion caught light. Lee would not talk to Tony though. Tim noticed that, after George went back to his catering duties, Lee was quietly humming and singing and steadily increasing the volume of this to block out Tony's attempts to prise him open for information and views. Tony eventually ceased and retreated to another table. One of the assistants joined in humming and singing with Lee, as did Tim, and then Lee added his own rhythm accompaniment, hands beating out sharply on the table.

George shouted over: 'You know Lee, you should record that. I ain't 'eard it since I was a lad. Always loved it...can't get hold of it nowhere.'

He went over and turned off the cafe sound system as a few more customers and his two assistants were now singing along as they served dishes, guessing the lyrics, but then belting out the chorus.

Tim went to have a word with Tony to ask whether he would entertain the idea of making a recording of Lee and offered to pay for it.

'You know like a basic field recording, I think they call it.'

Tony shrugged: 'Yea, that would be cool...but who's going to persuade him? It would only cost the price of a CD...that's not the problem.'

When George heard about the idea, he was forthright. He would be able to successfully work on Lee and was excited about having a resident artist in the cafe. As he said, there could be more hidden gems to come from Lee.

The following week, a few days before Christmas, Tim walked into this cafe corner of the Caribbean and George greeted him. He held up a shiny CD.

'Hey Father, man, wait till you hear this!'

Lee's voice was surprisingly strong, set against a simple yet compelling rhythm section. It rang out, filling the cafe with its smoky tone. A little brass had been added to pep up the track. Tim looked over to Lee's place and sure enough the man himself was there, beaming away, singing along.

'With Tony and Lee's permission, I sent a copy off to Radio Manchester with a note and, guess what, they say they will play it on Christmas Eve and Christmas Day!'

'Well I don't know what to say George, except fantastic. Well done! You should be very proud of what you've done for your Dad's old pal. I'm sure he would...'

'What? Say again. What do you mean Tim? Who's this old pal of Dad's ...'cause it ain't Lee? Where you get that from?'

'Oh right. Sorry I must have...'

'Thing is see...Lee comes in here, couple o'years back an'...well, he was practically beggin'...in a wretch'd state. I do not know him from Adam, notatall...but I do not wanna him starve, for sure.'

Put Out To Sea

'Here we are at last!' announced the coach driver as he pulled up the handbrake. The raucous singing of 'We do like to be beside the seaside' stopped abruptly.

A child cried out, 'Is this it? Where's the sea? Mam, I can't see the sea!'

A teenager stated categorically that this was a dump and it wasn't Blackpool.

'All the way from Manny...for this.'

Lydia thought one of the mothers on the back row had made this last comment.

They were neatly parked at Southport right at the front, only a low wall separating the huge empty carpark tarmac from the beach. The sterility of the scene shocked Lydia. Her mate, Kate, wanted to know why the place was deserted.

Lydia scanned the far distant horizon hoping for a glimpse of sea, whilst Kate and a couple of others stepped down off the coach into the drizzle to light their roll-ups. Somewhere, Kate assured them, there was a seashore, complete with crashing waves, it lay far beyond the dingy beach that they could see set out before them, in every direction an endless expanse of grimy looking lino.

All was not lost yet though for this Ladybarn Summer Playscheme 1977 grand finale. Thumping pop music could be heard. It reached out to the thirty strong party, heralding a fairground at the far end of the carpark. Donna Summer's big hit blared out, followed by 'Lonely Boy'. Not welcomed by Lydia.

'Oh no not Andrew gagging Gold again.'

The teenagers were caught by the upbeat this brought and most were already beginning to drift in the direction of the pleasure dome. The drizzle clung to bare arms and legs exposed in summer outfits, soaking 'T' shirts and shorts. Kate caught their mood and was prompted to yell:

'Come on Lyd let's get out of this pisshole. At least it will be dry over there.'

Lydia, the paid playscheme leader, called everyone to attention. They sheltered behind the back of the coach to hear her deliver her orders.

'We leave precisely at five pm. Have you got that? Not five past five, but five on the dot. If you are late...well, sorry, but you find your own way back home...all by yourself. I mean it, you'll be on your own. We can't wait for you. We won't wait for you!' Kate offered to chase after the departed teenagers to remind them.

It was an unspoken understanding between them that Kate, much to Lydia's frustration, was far more comfortable talking with these teenagers. They both knew why. Perhaps thought Lydia, I'll learn the knack. She hung back to chat with a few of the older teenagers and adults, and heard herself, with a chill, sounding too much like her Dad, a headmaster.

The mass exodus of around thirty fun-seekers to the fairground were offered only a few brief thrills. After less than half an hour funds had fizzled out, spends blown away on candyfloss and short rides. However, by now the drizzle had dried up and the sky lightened. Stella, a mother of two and a friend of Lydia and Kate, led the charge, storming the beach with several strollers rolling out behind her onto the firm wet sand.

On the beach sandcastles had been hatched, and one or two were under siege from jealous siblings and cheeky rivals. Kate could just about be seen. She had set off into the distance with a small expeditionary party determined to find and jump into the sea. Lydia was pleased that Stella appeared upbeat and relaxed remembering the frazzled figure she had first met in the launderette in Ladybarn a few months ago. On that occasion, Stella had rushed out suddenly with her toddler, Mary, who was dribbling sick. Later, returning, after she had found a neighbour to mind Mary for a few moments, she had thanked Lydia for cleaning up the vomit and sorting out her washing.

'I only moved your washing into the dryer, it was no bother. Honest.'

'How much do I owe you?' had started a rather awkward conversation, but ended well enough for them to enjoy a long chat when they next met in the corner shop. At another encounter in the launderette Stella had asked Lydia to recommend a book to read from amongst the items lining the shelf below the soap powder and tablet dispenser, marked 'book swop'. Stella commented that she seemed to spend a lot of time in the place because, with Connor being five and Mary two, there was always the washing. Also, her machine was permanently on the blink, had been for some time and what with Mary's potty training only a work in progress...'

'Anyhow...you'd know better being at college an' all that, what's good.'

What Lydia did know was that she could irritate friends by being pedantic, so didn't inform Stella that she had in fact graduated, as it was grandly termed, with a degree in History not English Literature. Quickly she had suggested 'Jaws', which she'd not read, rather than 'Catch 22', the book she'd donated on her last visit.

The launderette impressed Kate and Lydia. There were all manner of ads and notices displayed. Some were simply scrawled on torn scraps, others typed, cleverly illustrated and laminated. Work and services were on offer at reasonable rates, a final flourish usually claiming that no job was too small. You could browse over a diverse range of items for sale at bargain prices, and offer for goods which were often described as being in first rate condition. Clubs were always looking out for new members. Hiking groups, Mums and Tots, yoga sessions, fishing outings. You could catch the latest allotment updates, glance at the parish newsletter, or GUS catalogues and well-thumbed magazines.

'It acts as an embryo community centre,' Kate would say to all and sundry, sounding pleased with herself, the sociology graduate, now studying nursing. 'It provides a source of useful and relevant information, an informal network for the council estate.'

Not that Ladybarn was all council tenants. Lydia and Kate lived in a flat in a substantial if decaying villa around the corner where there were a few Edwardian and large Victorian dwellings, now mostly flats. The council estate was bordered by streets of terraced Victorian housing. Sitting in The Ladybarn, an end of terrace pub building, reminded Kate, she often said, of being in her great grandma's front room, with plenty of odd brass items and prized pieces of china on display.

It was Stella, on yet another visit to the launderette, who was always looking for bargain buys, who had spotted the card advertising the six-week Playscheme Leader post. She passed on the message to Lydia and Kate.

Lydia was interested, but Kate was fully occupied with her nurse training course.

'I've got to start earnin' Lyd, use my degree to get me a decent job, a career. Don't look so surprised...we weren't all born with silver spoons stuck in our gob...sorry, you're blushing...like that time your old man dipped his hand in his pocket and slipped us some dosh so we could get a square meal inside us for once, he said...and it was enough to feed a bleeding family of four for a fortnight! That was a laugh. What a bender that was! Anyway...this playscheme lark would suit you, at this present moment in time, as they say.'

Lydia had been signing-on now for a few weeks whilst she was supposed to be thinking about her future plans. Kate had warned her that it was intended to be a humiliating experience for the poor sod signing-on. Lydia had found it grim but not entirely demeaning. After all, it was only temporary for her, hardly onerous and broadened her experience.

For example, the actual Labour Exchange performance of standing in a windowless subterranean hall in three long lines, the appropriate one determined by where your surname fell alphabetically, was only required once a week. You waited to reach the counter to sign your name to release your cheque, at the same time, each and every week. Or you went without. This provided Lydia with the opportunity to meet and greet other shipmates and pretend they were all in the same lifeboat. She enjoyed their cynical witticisms and joined in with the sarcastic guffaws. One stayed with her over the years: 'Have you seen the news...there's plenty of jobs in jeopardy...but, do you know how to get there?'

One upright claimant of ample form was unforgettable. A dishevelled, unshaven, grizzly gent in a grossly oversized coat with greasy lapels, who always arrived and departed courtesy of a taxi. It was said that a mate or relative, an obliging black-cab driver, conveyed him door-to-door, back and forth without fail every week. His long lank hair was slicked back behind his ears and lay limply over his collar, yet he carried himself in a stately manner as if he was the Lord Mayor.

On every occasion that Lydia saw him, this claimant strode in, carefully and triumphantly carrying a small, dirty, battered cardboard box, opened out to reveal three or four large cream cakes. Invariably he made sure, at the exact moment when he berthed at the counter to face the clerk, that he had an enormous mouthful stuffed in his cakehole.

Lydia was standing alongside him once in her line-up and noticed, on being asked to confirm, once again, his name, address and date of birth, sprays of cream spattering forth, whilst he offered one of the delicacies to the clerk by shoving it under her nose. Unsurprisingly, this generous act was declined. Lydia wondered how fresh the cakes actually were when you saw them close up. It was all, according to Kate, an act of mild defiance.

So Lydia was treading water when the Playscheme post appeared, babysitting for Stella and shopping and cooking for Kate. Kate had managed to arrange a free day to help with the Southport trip.

On the beach, Lydia watching all the children happy playing and with the full sun emerging, was moved to comment, 'Stella it must be lovely...fulfilling I mean...you must have a real sense of purpose...you know...bringing up your children. I wonder whether...'

'What do mean Lyd? It's totally knackering and, well, bloody boring at times. Oh don't get me wrong, I love the little blighters...I wouldn't be without them, I love them to bits, but...well, I miss the girls at McVities...and the ginger nuts.' She started giggling. 'Sorry that's a bit of a joke from the factory... you see...well...I haven't anyone to help...what with Mam working and their father having buggered off. Disappeared for good...and I do mean good, if you know what I mean.'

Whilst her children were immersed in soggy sand building castles and dams, Stella rolled a cigarette, lit it, and turning to Lydia asked her:

'Have you been here before?'

'No. Bit bleak isn't it?...actually, we always went to the east coast for family holidays.'

'Oh yeah...Brid or Scarborough...?'

'Whitby, mostly, or Filey...they liked quiet resorts...'

'Dead posh you mean!'

Smiling, Stella heaved herself up and went over to sort out an outbreak of sibling sand throwing while Lydia thought of Whitby...she possessed a hoard of happy memories, such as racing her brother up the 199 steps past the Georgian church hunkered on the headland, the ruins of the ancient abbey overlooking the piers, a pair of giant pincers guarding the harbour. Remember the catch at the back of your throat near the smokehouse under the cliff...Oh and how earnest they had been as children crabbing by the swing bridge... and worrying that her little brother would topple over the side. Fantastic fish and chips...done the Yorkshire way. And she had always enjoyed skipping between the incoming tidal surges sucking at your feet as you scrunched your way up to Sandsend, a dripping ice-cream your reward. Not forgetting about going in the opposite direction...ambling along the cliff tops to Robin Hood's Bay... searching for fossils. Taking the bus back, sat on the top deck.

So rich her store...the shops showing shiny coal jet jewellery. Her Mum naming elegant waders with insect-thin legs...and the fulmars, her favourite, making comical attempts to land on ledges, failing a few times but finally persisting. On stormy moonlight nights her Dad would tell Dracula-like tales... well any night if he felt like it. And of course, the daily swimming in what could be a millpond sea, or when the waves were huge and scary.

Then Stella was abruptly shouting beside her.

'Connor Maguire, I've just told you to stop it...any more throwing sand and we go home...now...no treats!'

'I've always thought Stella...well...that's a hell of a name to live up to, you know. Connor Maguire.'

'What you saying Lyd? I don't get you. What do you mean, luv? It was his Dad, Liam, you know who came up with it...before he finally effed off.'

'A student of Irish history was he?'

'Well, he would do very well on that Mastermind or University Whatsit... if the questions were all on say, boozing or betting odds...or how the Brits have done the Irish down for hundreds and hundreds of years...on and on about it... anyway, tell me all about Connor.'

'Well, in 1640 or thereabouts...well, let's just say...a certain Connor Maguire came to a rather sticky end. He was a rebel and was executed...quite a hero.'

'Oh, I didn't know that...I do remember Liam going on about the bold Fenian men. I thought he was saying, the bald Fenians and, well, I could never work out what losing your hair had to do with, you know...the struggle for independence. The devious bastard Brits he would often say. Used to moan about people at work saying the IRA are all scum and the Irish...well, just a load of thick-as-shit Micks. His old man was the same in a way, not moaning but...well...he were always singing the old rebel songs... 'The Croppy Boy'...do you know it? It's a great song mind. Oh and the sad, so sad story of poor Leo Casey...I don't know if that makes his son a student of anything much...

'Listen, Stella, I've got lots of good books on Irish history, it's really inter-esting...do you want to...'

'Oh no. I could never...thanks though. As I say Liam's Da was a great one for Irish tales and songs of the Troubles...a lovely man, don't know why Liam couldn't have been more like him...he had some great stories to tell, his Da. He was well known for it. Had it all stored away up here...in his head. Me Mam sang a lot of Irish songs too, now I think about it. I liked the singing. I used to join in and she loved that. Her Dad was quite a hothead too, or his family were...he were in some union or political something. Died fairly young though...cancer. Mam used to do the dancing too...an' was always trying to get me and our Eileen to go...you know, to the Irish Centre, but we weren't having it. She still goes at her age...just for the chitchat now.'

Lydia suggested to Stella that she probably knew a lot already as the folk songs and ballads were a rich source of information. 'We studied them on our course. They tell you loads...and you already, probably, know more than me...'

Stella shrugged, then smiled.

'It would be good to piece it all together Stella. You know, try and make sense of events...what the songs are saying, it could be fun...what I'm trying to say is that it's not all boring textbook study you know...there's the music, the newspapers of the time and the handbills, and letters and stories and stuff. You could talk to your Mum about it. Some people like to trace their family history.'

When summer and the Playscheme were well and truly over in mid-September, Lydia found further paid work at the Eighth Day, a co-operatively run restaurant, bakery and shop in All Saints, deep in Manchester student land. They were prepared to offer her the opportunity to wash up a lot. Also clear tables and wait on, when required. Remuneration was modest but it meant an end to signing on. Eighth Day was on Europe's busiest bus route, one cus-tomer had told her, but for Lydia, it was only a short bike ride from Ladybarn through Rusholme. The interview, which she had prepared for meticulously, including asking Kate to help her rehearse likely questions, had turned out to be merely a two-minute chat, mainly about what music and food she enjoyed.

Lydia liked the place and the people. She hung out there in her time off and on Saturdays, when not working, would meet up with a gaggle of friends. Kate joined them when she could.

One day Lydia went round to see Stella with a proposal.

'Stella let's go up town tomorrow. We're having an open day at Eighth Day... a party! You can see where I work and there will be loads of fun things for the kids to do. We've booked a children's entertainer and there's a crèche. There's some folk singing...and musicians coming too.'

'It won't be like those druggy festivals and wild student parties you told me about, will it?'

'No, not likely! We've got our licence to think of and there should be a lot of children. We are trying to attract more families.' Realising she had forgotten a sure-fire selling point, she quickly added: 'Oh, and there will be free food of course and we can bring our own booze. I've got a couple of bottles for us to take. They'll have squash for the kids.'

Once inside Eighth Day, Connor and Mary Maguire made their way with Lydia straight over to the soft-play ballpark and face-painting, whilst Stella wandered over to a corner set up as an impromptu performance space where a woman was singing an enchanting song, accompanying herself on guitar. Then an older bearded man joined her for more lively numbers. He finished by saying that they had learnt this last tune from a friend who didn't know anything about its origins. As he and his partner walked past Stella on their way to the food, Stella blurted out that she knew the song was from Cavan where it was called 'The Restless Maid.' It was a favourite of her father-in-law. The couple were intrigued and returned to eat their buffet with Stella to find out what she knew.

'Oh, that's all I know actually. Sorry.'

'What part of Cavan does he hail from? Have you been there?'

Kate arrived shortly after finishing her shift. She found Lydia with the children and then noticed Stella deep in conversation with a small group all eating and drinking wine. Afterwards, waiting for the bus Stella was brimming over: 'That was great...thanks for thinking of us... inviting us an' all.' Her smile was wide and took in Kate, Lydia and a fair few at the bus stop. 'That couple I was rabbiting on to...well, they want me to start going to their, uh... folk club evenings. At 'The Grey Mare'...in Shudehill, if you know it.'

Upstairs on the bus going home, passing the Hollins Catering College, Kate couldn't resist telling Connor that the pair of buildings they had stopped outside and were looking over, were known as the toast rack and poached egg.

'It's a sort of joke, Con. Imagine a giant's breakfast table perhaps. Do you see it...there's the toast rack. Do you not know what a toast rack is?' Turning to Lydia, she mumbled, 'Anyway...it's only a modernist piece of make-believe me thinks'.

Lydia, very much preoccupied, asked Stella: 'Why not start going to the folk club? You know one of us could always babysit?' Kate nodded. Stella frowned.

'Oh I dunno. Tony was easy to get along with but she's rather la-di-da... don't be fooled by the denim jacket...she lives in Didsbury I'll have you know. They did get me to chat with this other couple who go, and they're ok...quiet like me. An' Tony says there's a few who like to sing the Irish songs.'

'There you go...and that Tony was trying to interest us...it's only once a fortnight.'

Lydia and Kate, as far as they could, took it in turns to accompany Stella to the Grey Mare. In fact it was usually the highlight of the month for whoever went out on the town with Stella, although both of them enjoyed story time and cuddles with the children as the alternative.

One night on the lurching late-night bus back from the boozy singing session, Stella couldn't stop herself stumbling out with an observation.

'Kate, I hope you don't mind me saying ...you and Lyd...I don't get it...how come you two get on so well, but you're so different, like in where you come from, I mean...Lyd's from some swanky home with rich parents and all that, and...well, you've had to graft to get here, do Saturday jobs...and there's your Dad been put out of work for yonks...your Mam takes on extra cleaning jobs and...you said you're the first in your family to go to college.'

'I know, but you see Lyd's...the thing is...she's the one who got me through it all...I wasn't coping to begin with, first week I felt...felt homesick basically... you know... out of place...and she built me up and sort of pulled me along with her...we always had a bloody good laugh...from day one, fresher's week. There were a lot of loud-mouthed prats, all privileged and sneery...but we found a few people that were ok, some like me...I liked Lyd a lot before I knew just how grand her folks were. She used to tell me: don't let any sod here grind you down.'

'Right...an' now after all that studying you're both getting your hands dirty, so to speak...doing hands-on stuff...fancy you sluicing shitty bed-pans and ...she's forever washing-up and clearing dishes, by the sounds of it...'

'Actually, Lydia's considering doing something more serious now. Might go teaching or working abroad. She says it's high time she put out to sea, left the safety of the shore...set sail...she makes me laugh when she comes out all poetic! Had enough of slumming it, I ask her...just to tease her, you know.'

'I hope she's not going to try to set sail from Southport!'

'Ha, no, not bloody likely. Be easier at Salford! And quicker! Anyway the point is...I'm still studying. I like the nursing 'cause I can apply what I'm learn-ing. It's hard...but you want to learn how to get it right for the sake of the poor old patients...in fact I'm on the ward tomorrow being observed. The focus is on writing up obs. Oh, sorry that's...observations...I'll have to know my stuff tomorrow...and have clean hands and a spotless uniform. Anyway, if I can do it...I keep thinking maybe you should...you know, start thinking Stella about perhaps...going back to work, or education...listen that reminds me, Lyd and I have found this great women's group...you could come with us. Oh and there's a crèche...'

Stella listened patiently, but then asked: 'Hey, that reminds me – how you doing with that fella of yours?'

'Don't change the subject! And he's ok but it's nothing heavy...nothing serious, honest. No, I mean it. It's Lyd I think who most needs some deep TLC after being pushed aside by that bastard Frank creature.'

'That's a shame...same old story eh, left high and dry while the so and so swans off, or sods off more like. So what do you talk about, when you're not moaning about bloody fellahs...in this women's thingy?'

'Well there is time for doing all that in the breaks...if you want...there's good support for personal issues. Easy to make friends, I'd say. It's helping me a lot...but at the moment we are on about education and sharing skills and knowledge and overcoming feelings of inferiority...they have this thingy bob called becoming assertive.'

'Sounds a bit serious Kate...anyway I haven't got much in the way of skills to share...unless toilet training toddlers counts.'

'Yea well, it might help someone there...but ugh, look how you've helped Tony with some of those Irish tunes he wants to learn and Lyd says you've been looking at the Irish history stuff she lent you...asking her lots of questions.'

'That's because I know so little and understand even less. I like that beginner's guide one with funny cartoons. It is interesting...'specially compared with washing, cleaning, shopping, cooking...Oh look out, this is our stop, don't want to miss it, next one's bloody miles.'

The following Saturday afternoon, Stella made a surprise call on Lydia and Kate with the children in tow. They were urged to come in and the children surged in excited and rushed up to the flat.

'We've had our tea, hope we're not interrupting yours. I just need to talk, tell you stuff, but first...Lyd, tell me...it's none of my business...but Kate told me you're thinking of sacking the Eighth Day and teaching Teflon or Tessa or something...I'm worried Lyd ...you'll be off going to live somewhere else...I'll miss you luvvie!'

'Oh yea, I was thinking of TESL or EFL, teaching English as a...anyway, never mind me. What's up Stella? You look like you've been through the mangle. You said you needed to talk?'

'I am—

I had a visit, you see. From Liam...the other night...hang on, Connor put that down...now!'

'I'll get those conkers, fir cones they like Lyd, oh and the saucepans and pots. They can make us their hearty autumn stew again. Carry on Stella.'

'Here, I'll give you a hand. I've got their yo-yos here...'

'I don't think they feature in an autumn stew Stella...oh, apparently they do, along with dice and chess pieces. Right, that's better. You were saying about Liam...I take it you weren't expecting to see him.'

'Too bloody right...not at all...came completely out the blue. Sneaky bastard. Course he was dead drunk. But he took me by surprise you see. Just shoved his way in, before I ...yea it was frightening at first but then he tried to turn on the charm...doesn't work on me anymore. Oh he wanted so much for us to get back together, oh how he misses the kids...he said...well, he hasn't been in touch for eighteen months!'

Lydia put the kettle on. Kate sat down next to Stella. They both looked at her expectantly, willing her to continue.

'I told him to go, get lost for good... an' that I was seeing someone. Someone I'd met at the folk club. I know, I know, it's misleading, stringing him along, but...needs must. What do they call it...a white lie? Wait. Wait...there's more...I said that I am heavily into a women's group...that, uh, oh I'm studying part-time... haven't got no time, or the slightest bleeding interest Liam at the nothing you could offer me or the kids... I really laid it on thick that I'd got a new life, a better life...I panicked, but do you know...it worked! He went dead quiet. He couldn't even look me in the eye. So...right...the point is Lydia, Kate...I've made my mind up...I am going to start going...going to that Women's Lib thing...if they'll have me. That's why I've come round actually...I need to know more...like, how to go about it.'

'That's great. We'll show you. We will take you!'

'Yea it is, a great idea Stella. Really positive. What else do you want us to do?'

'I hope you don't mind, the both of youse, but... I'm sorry... like I say I was in a blind panic, got carried away...I went an' gave him this address to call at if he didn't believe me. Called his bluff. I know...it's a bit of a story...you could say I've been unfair to him, I guess...But I can't stand the thought...And with a little help from you two, I could give it a go you know! Launch meself, you might say. Leave the safety of the shore. Scary.' She looked up to see Kate grinning.

'That's a good way to put it,' Lydia agreed.

'Any road, in the meantime, will you tell him till the bugger understands... that it's true...if he ever shows his ugly mug here...you know, say I'm doing these things...you can make him get the message, he's history...cause I've changed...everything's different...so much has changed! I don't think he's at all likely to come round...he'll be too scared. But this should get rid of him once and for all. Oh, you should have seen his face when he slunk out!'

Kate replied first, 'Of course we will. You know you can count on us. We'll back you up...and it's not telling tales. You can do it!'

Sharpened Pennies

Jim and Dave thought the journey to the footie, rolling around stuck in the back of Wardy's tatty Transit van was bad enough, but standing trapped in the packed crowd in the Kippax at Filbert Street ten minutes after kick-off someone nearby had shouted 'Watch out...Missiles...incoming...sods are chucking stones'. Then a fan even closer muttered, 'No...it's sharpened pennies.' Leicester City, the Foxes were hosting the Tricky Trees, their arch-rivals, Nottingham Forest. Jim had one eye on the game, the other looking out for missiles.

Shielding their faces with arms raised the mates at least were able to savour Storey-Moore prodding at the ball, forcing it to inch towards the goal. It seemed to happen in slow motion, and you could swear you heard the ball gasp as it passed over the line beyond the outstretched legs of desperate defenders. The moment it dribbled into the net Forest fans exploded with joy. Jim thought what on earth had that teacher been on about with his daft Zeno's paradox, the arrow and the elusive target...the ball had reached the back of the net!

As they left the ground Wardy said they must find the van straightaway and check the tyres were still intact. Hurrying came as a relief to Jim with Dave acting as if he was still in enemy territory looking to take a few prisoners before they left. 'Cocky bleeders, I hate 'em.' Dave could be plainly embarrassing at times...after all one or two of the lads they hung out with at school supported City, or Derby.

Jim and Dave had been friends from way back, first in nursery, then primary school. They could recall enjoying sucking jubilees, playing marbles, conker fights and having fun with plasticine and papier mache. Through all the growing years they'd stuck together. Dave, a tall, stern boisterous child had turned into a truculent teenager whilst Jim favoured reflection and was more kindly disposed to the world they encountered. Dave had jumped off the school conveyor belt as soon as he could, aged fifteen years and ten months. With great relief he rushed off to work with his dad on the family market stalls in Loughborough and Leicester. Now when the lads met up they would chat about sex and drugs and rock 'n' roll. 'Wasn't Neil Young great...better than that maudlin James Taylor', was how Jim expressed it. Dave thought Taylor 'sad shit'. They had both been pleased to discover Loudon Wainwright and after a couple of pints of Watneys and sharing a joint, would bawl out the chorus of 'Dead skunk in the middle of the road'.

Back home, Jim told the tale of the score draw to his Dad, Ted, not mentioning the hostile, scary atmosphere except to say, 'It was heaving with cops Dad, swarming all over they were...never seen so many.'

'Right...you know if I hadn't been on overtime today son, I would have joined you, but Brush is generous with its overtime...mainly because management keep cocking things up, half the time we're standing around with very little to do, then they wake up an' there's an almighty panic. Les looks after me. Bit of extra for tonight an' all. We're off for a jar or two with him an' Lorraine. No surprises there eh? Hey, nearly forget to tell ya...we've got right big contracts coming up for transformers...from Russia, an' engines with British Rail.'

'Dad do you reckon you could get to be like Les, one of them...union stewards, or whatever it's called?'

'Why son?'

'Then we could live in a bigger house of course... like Les in Great Central Road...have an attic room and a little back garden...'

'Maybe. Not sure I'd want all that stress...an' any road our 'ouse is fine for three of us...an' I ain't bothered so long as we've an 'edge by front door...your mother 'as room to 'ang out washing in yard.'

'Suppose so.'

'By the way, did you take that friend of yours...that Nagjam lad to the game? No...well please don't tell me you didn't... didn't go in that bloody death trap of Ward's did you?'

'We did Dad. Dave and I, and a couple of others that Wardy knows.'

'How is Dave by the way? His Dad's having an 'ard time you know...Council want to charge them stallholders more.'

'He's fine...still real glad to have packed in school. Likes the work...moans a lot about the Asians though...goes on and on about Pakis. Never seems to stop...like it's driven him round the bend.'

'What the stallholders?'

'Yea them some...but mainly the customers...says they're always out to haggle...says they're all dead snidey...and smelly... and want to do you down... or do him down any rate, take advantage like.'

'Well...he needs to understand... it's just their custom...their way of doing things. It's what they do...what they're used to...I remember it were like that out Aden way, I seen it...and happens in Kenya I believe. You know...I don't know why we all don't do it! Haggle I mean. He wants to be far less stuck up his arse and...well, you can't say all their stuff is top notch now can ya? I'd want to feel it first, I can tell ya...you know, I'm sure half the bloody time them market traders look you over... and then make up a price they reckon you might pay...what they can get away with!'

After Les had finished mooching about the market, he turned the corner into the Leicester Road and came upon Jim and an Asian lad out from school and deep in conversation. He had to stand right in front of them before they noticed him.

'Ow do me ducks...now then Jim, what false pearls of wisdom have your so-called teachers being laying before you... you being real swine like!?'

'Oh yea...you're always saying that Les!...he always says the same Nag... then he always go on to say...education should be subversive...education should make you question things...schools don't teach you sweet f a...nowt useful about how the world works. They keep it all hidden, they do...them rich and powerful sods.'

'That's right. Well said! I couldn't agree with meself more! Now then, who's this Jim?'

'Oh, ok...this is Nagjam'

'Hi, pleased to meet you mate...where did you spring from, fellah?'

'Oh...I'm from near here actually, down that street there...Russell Street... do you know it?'

'Of course. Been there long?...I mean here long...how?...'

'About... five years.'

'Yea right, I see...but where are you from?...in which... know what I mean...?'

'What he means Nag, is where do you come from originally?'

'Of course Jim I know when people ask me this wur ya frum business... well what they really want to know is this...that I came from Kenya in 1965. My parents moved there, to that part of Africa, from India. I am British...my passport says I am ...'

'Sure, sure...steady on. I didn't mean anything...it's tough out there now ain't it...if you ain't African, I suppose.'

'It is. My Dad was telling me not long ago that we just had to leave. I was only ten.'

'I see. Tough shit eh. But weren't you allowed to stay...become a native...I mean...become Kenyan?'

'Yes we could, but...well no, no... see they made it very hard. Definitely made it clear they wanted us out. That's what Dad says.'

'Any road...pleased to meet you lad and...well I may see you again soon Jim...I'm off to call on your ol' man before I start me late shift. See you lads.'

They watched Les walk off briskly, and ambled along in his wake. 'Who's he Jim?'

'Oh, Les. Big mate of me Dad. From work. Always talking to Dad about their rights at work and how to stand up to the bosses...political sort of stuff I suppose...brings around newspapers...not the sort you get in shops... and leaflets... even booklet things for Dad to read. I look at 'em. Dad can't be bothered much.'

'Do you like him?'

'I do. He's a grafter...always trying to learn. That's why he goes on about school being a waste of space. He often says, I've had to educate meself. I think he's quite clever. He wants me to go to college...and he goes to lots of courses with the union. He tells me that he don't know anyone who's been to the colleges of knowledge. He means university or polys. You go Jim, he'll say, then you can tell me what it's like.'

'That's good. Has he family, or...'

'There's just him and his missus, Lorraine...they go out boozing with Mum and Dad most weekends. Come to think of it, Lorraine works at that mill near you...the one in Trinity Street...me Mum worked there before I were born. Any road...right listen Nag...got to see a man about a dog...well, I mean I'm off to see Dave. He'll be at his stall...and I'll see thee tomorrow...ta for your help with that Physics...reporting the experiment. I can write it up now. Thanks.'

'Hang on a minute Jim, I meant to ask you...did you watch the match, on the telly. The Forest one. I bet that's...uh, well, interesting...you know, watching it on the box after you've been to the game?'

'It's strange yea...funny what they cut out... or leave in, what you remember, what you didn't notice at the match or have forgotten...the different view, it's a funny angle...you can't see all the uhm...the whole thing...it feels flat actually, not like actually being there...not as exciting as if it's actually happening, if you know what I mean. Difficult to explain...'

'Must have been great. I'd love to go...anyway, see ya.'

When he arrived at the market, Dave was pleased to see Jim and came around the front of the stall to sound off.

'That bleeding red Les has been winding me up Jim. The bugger was banging on about how much better Rams are than Forest this season...saying our manager's crap...oh hang on, see that, that Paki's fingering everything.'

'Wow, Dave, stay cool, man...make the sale...customer relations an' all that.'

'Yea right, but it makes me feel sick...'

'But don't most people want to handle...feel for quality...or is it that what worries you?'

'Ha, bloody ha. Look she's running her greasy...slimy hands over everything.'

'How can you tell they're...Oh jus' don't keep goin' on about it...please.' Jim reintroduced the progress of Derby County to change the subject.

'Never mind that...are you still seeing that Convent bird Jim?'

'Nah. Kicked her into touch. Think we bored each other...wasn't going anywhere, if ya know what I mean.'

'Could have told ya...not the type.'

Jim walked slowly home, partly thinking about what Nag had said on how to approach that homework task, but also trying not to dwell on Dave's uncalled for remarks. What was it with Dave? He was fast becoming a bore on the subject for one thing. Bloody obsessed...a sickness.

He thought back to when he'd first met Nagjam. At the start of secondary school when there had been this surprise appearance of a brown face. Jim had been fascinated. A visitor from an exotic world, from the so-called Dark Continent of Africa. Dark Continent...did they never have the lights on, did the sun never shine? Nag had from that first day been a model of grooming. With his polished-looking jet black hair, he glided along unruffled in his uniform, which actually fitted, and he was able to follow all the bizarre new rules to the letter, often having to explain the intricacies of the timetable to other boys in that first fortnight. Not that he had any friends in the class but knocked around at break with one older pupil and a teacher's son the same age but in another class.

In the English composition class on the theme of 'first impressions' the teacher had encouraged Nagjam to read out his effort about arriving in Loughborough from Kenya aged ten. He had written that he was surprised to see white men emptying the bins and sweeping the streets, and that in winter you could see your own breath like steam.

As the terms and years rolled along Jim grew to enjoy Nag's conversation especially about science topics and news, but only possessed the scantiest details about his home life as he hadn't wanted to be nosey. By their fifth year they had become firm friends and often chose to pair up for science experiments. Nag seemed to Jim to be a refreshing contrast to Dave. He was far more open-minded, lively and thoughtful.

'I like to think things out for myself Jim, you know.'

One afternoon in Biology they were introduced to the science topic of the so-called Green Revolution. The teacher had explained the science behind the development of more disease resistant seeds and crops which enabled greater self-sufficiency and independence for poorer parts of the underdeveloped world. Or so it was claimed by vested interests, Nag warned Jim after the lesson. The teacher had been very enthusiastic about it all, but to Nag's way of thinking had skated over the various political and ethical considerations and these were just, or even more important than the technical issues.

To help with the choice of 'A' levels the school offered Careers Advice sessions. Chatting after one of these Nag told Jim of his Dad's frustrations with the lab assistant job and how his Dad was looking to study to advance. Also his Mum, with his sisters now in school, had started working a few shifts in the Trinity Street hosiery mill around the corner from their home. She too had ambitions. She wanted to be trained as a skilled worker. Ambitious, not like his own parents, Jim thought.

Next day, reflecting on what it must have been like to be Nag, an Indian having to leave Africa to come to Europe, to come to England ending up in Loughborough, he had to ask:

'You know Nag you were telling Les the other day about leaving Kenya... Have I got this right...that you...well, you weren't exactly kicked out of Kenya, but more made to feel, ugh, very unwelcome?'

'Yes they made damn sure they made us feel unwelcome, not wanted at all, it put us on edge all the time, but listen...I'm just repeating what my Dad has told me...even though he doesn't like talking about it I keep nagging to know more. I was just a little kid and lived in a little Indian world...a sort of Hindu bubble, I think now. I had no idea what was kicking off.'

'But you could have stayed?'

'You could if you became a citizen, which meant giving up your British passport, paying a load of dosh and even after all that...well, then they could just take away your Kenyan citizenship...anytime, for any reason. Then you'd be right up shit creek. My Uncle...see, he did stay on...he sent Dad a letter last month 'cause he wants out now... he knows friends whose applications have somehow got lost or ignored. Never received, officials say... start again, please. I'm so glad now that we got out early. I'm not annoyed with Dad so much now!'

'What about going...couldn't you move to another country nearby, uh, like uh....oh I dunno. Any good?'

'Huh, you are joking! Dad says there was this other family last year tried to get over to Uganda. They were refused entry. Ended up being kicked from Entebbe to London. London says you can't come in go back to Entebbe. Uganda then sends them back to Nairobi...so they tried again, flying in to London, refused again...sent back to Kenya...get this...who passed them on to Uganda...you get the picture!.'

'Shit. Pass the homeless people parcel. What happened ...where are they now?'

'Oh right...here in the UK...UK took them in the end. They were British citizens...same as you and me after all!'

'Did your family, or any of your friends, ever think of going back to India?'

'If only...but the Blessed Mrs Gandhi said she didn't want us...unless, well it's complicated, I'm not sure...says basically we're British, let your Wilson or Heath sort it out...not her problem. And of course we've been welcomed here like...well, sewage washed up on a clean beach! Les is right...it's a bit tough.'

Jim had never heard such bite in Nag's tone, bitter and angry.

It was Saturday night at *The Peacock*. Ted and Les had shot off to the pool room in the back clutching their second pints of Marston's.

Jan asked Lorraine for a penny for her thoughts, old or new decimal.

'It's work...'

'But you did brill last year ...threatening to strike and getting, what was it... oh, ten percent!'

'Of course, yes, that was fantastic Jan. Trouble is they're hitting back at us now, I was telling Les. They keep asking us to take on more and more of these new designs, dead awkward to do. Takes a lorra time to finish a piece.'

'But hang on...don't you get the Auxiliaries, them Asians to do 'em. You always used to. I know it's only piecework rates for them, but surely everyone's happy...if they come over here wanting the bloody work...they settle for it... and you don't want the hassle of them new designs...and management save loads of dosh paying piece-rate peanuts...well, everyone's a winner!'

'Managers not happy, that's the point...less inclined to let us skilled perms off doing them new designs...plenty of the crap stuff still to be done at piece-rate. Plus one or two of the Indians have joined the union and started speaking up...you can even understand them...that's the last thing we need.'

'What's union saying?'

'Keeping stumm...keeping out of it...that's why I was telling Les. They need to do something soon.'

As the pool players have now re-joined their better halves, Les comments.

'Problem is Lorraine you've got a lot more competition from the Far East. And over here there's a move everywhere...Brush and everywhere it seems, to introduce more machinery, and you know automation...don't want unskilled ...they go first...surely that's one less worry for you Lorraine.'

Then he added: 'What I do want to know...you must tell me...if you hear anything about bods turning up, outsiders sniffing around...maybe speaking to your Asian lot...'

'Like at Crepe Size you mean...it went on there I believe...a lot of outsiders sneakin' in...giving out advice...but Les that were different...an' the Pakis or Indians whoever...they came out in full support of rest of the workers there. On the pickets.'

The following Friday, Nag and Jim are homeward bound.

Nag asks: 'What you doing tomorrow?'

'Oh, not sure yet.'

'Aren't you going to the footie...Forest?'

'Maybe, yea could do...yea, probably.'

'I wouldn't mind going. Make a change from Match of the Day.'

'Right. Forest are great at the moment.'

'Playing Spurs...be a good game I think, loads of goals...how do you go now…?'

'How do you mean?'

'Well are you planning to travel by car, bus or with Wardy?'

'Not Wardy. His van's in need of a service he says…probably you know, the final one…the funeral. Dave and I…we are likely to get the bus. Depends really,. If Dad wants to come, we can cadge a lift in his mate Tony's Mini.'

'So could I…?'

'Nag …you know the score…you always know all the scores!…it's Dave, you know what he's like and if we were all squashed up that car…?'

'I don't mind him.'

'Yea, but…look, I'm sorry…he's more than likely you know to be…and there's lots of lads like Dave at games looking for trouble…shouting, chanting vile racist abuse…be like having sharpened pennies hurled at you. I'd worry…'

'Don't worry Jim. It's all right on the telly… and it's warm and dry. No standing about freezing on the terraces.'

This was awkward. It would be fun to go with Nag and share his delight. And he owed him bigtime for all his homework help. Nag was a good friend now. Someone he spent a lot of time with. He enjoyed calling round his place for what his Mum called 'chitchat and a cup of chai'. Nagjam's younger sisters sweetly smiling and milling around made him wish a little that he had sisters or at least a brother.

But there was no knowing what Dave would say or do. He might go completely batshit crazy, be very aggressive. Or totally mardy, never speaking to Jim ever again. He now realised what should have been obvious: he couldn't keep Dave and Nag at arm's length from each other for much longer. Did this mean he must choose between them? Was it a certainty that the three of them couldn't somehow rub along together? How come he had ended up with this headache?

On New Year's Eve Jim and his parents were invited to Les and Lorraine's party.

Lorraine was sounding off to Les and Jim, supping their beer, about the recent strike at Mansfield Mills. It had been in all the papers, even the national news on telly.

'It's over, finished, thank the Lord…'

'Everyone came to their senses…'

'Yea, finally, but for a while it was a right fucking madhouse what with them Asian girls at Trinity just walking out…no notice, no warning…just upped and stormed off. Marched down the bloody High Street…bold as bloody brass right up to union office…singing their heads off, all them chants, them santras or whatever ...actually it's quite funny now when I think about it! Made union sit up...take notice.'

'Mantras...I think you mean, luv.'

'Thanks professor Les...wasn't funny though when they said we were racialistic...telling tales to union...said we was always telling 'em to shurrup when they had grievances.'

'Yea well management did ignore the technical problems on new designs, Lorraine...an' did pay auxiliaries very poor rates... an' suspend 'em for days at the drop of a hat. Not right.'

'There you go Les with all your shop steward talk.'

'They were dead right though...and they needed proper representation...'

'They'd no idea about Unions when they cum here...bloody ignorant lot. Need to damn well learn English ways for a kick-off...and our lingo.'

'Well that can happen now. It's in the agreement. English classes...lessons learnt, you might say.'

'So it's all ok now? Will it all stay settled down now?' Jim asked.

'Oh I can't deny Jim it's better, far less us and them. All came out, stayed out...solid we were. It's good, I suppose...at least we're not bloody swearing at each other now.'

'We've got to change Jim,' Les added. 'See otherwise management will always find ways to divide and rule, always want to get their own way, do what they want. You young uns can lead the way...show 'em they can't keep doing it.'

'Ah Les, you're an old softie. Give us another drink, duck.'

Was that the turning point, listening to the chat with Lorraine and Les that persuaded Jim to ask Nag to come to the football with him? The next home game Dave couldn't attend, not match fit, had the flu. Nag had leapt at the chance.

He couldn't be sure, but he felt it probably was that coaching chat from Les that had made a difference.

A couple of months later it was clear that Dave didn't want anything more to do with Jim or his Dad.

'Hey Jim. I tell ya, bumped into Dave's dad outside post office and do you know what that rude git did? Completely blanked me...it shouldn't matter a monkey's that you two fell out big time...but...bloody mardy beggar.'

'Sorry Dad.'

'I seen him coming out and thought I'd tell him how great you're doing with that sandwich course at Trent Poly...earning while you're learning... might suit Dave I think. He could still live at home...oh I know he'd need night school first but...better than stuck for all time on that dead-end stall job.'

Oh well, sod him.'

'His choice, Dad.'

'Stupid not to...look at all these chances you kids have now...we never... listen, that reminds me...have you heard from young Nagjamy recently?'

'No, not for while...not since he was back for Diwali.'

'Oh yea...when he came round...doing right well at that there London college ain't he?'

'University, Dad.'

'So you say...Diwali tho' were months ago. Sorry son... you've no Dave...he's taken up with Wardy and those losers...and precious little Nag. Still...suppose it couldn't be helped.'

Battle for the Bogside

It had been a rude awakening after I'd been savouring glimpses of lush meadows and dappled woodland. One moment, as in a dream, catching sight of a young deer as our train sped past level crossings and a cute Victorian signal box. Full-on scenes of summer in East Yorkshire displaying the bold colours of David Hockney's recent work.

Then whilst standing to attention in Leeds station, a swarm of flying fucking fricatives invaded our quiet carriage as a dozen squaddies, let out on leave, all seeming to shout at once, careered up the aisle towards us. Carrying massive packs of lager, they were determined, they announced as if on the tannoy, to get completely fucking wasted and this mission was showing every sign of success with the constant guzzling of cans of lager and buzzing excited boasts of plans for living it up over their leave.

What must it be like to be seventeen or eighteen and serving in the army I wondered, but could only begin to reflect on this in the quiet after they had departed? Being drilled half the long day, having to salute every five minutes, strictly obeying all those rules and regulations, living in barracks far from home. In short, being at the total command and whim of others.

I found my thoughts drifting back over fifty years to when I was in the sixth form. My mate Tony was telling a few of us about his long-weekend careers visit to the Marines.

'I tell you the ale flowed. After a few pints we played this ace drinking game. They call it taking the piss...get this...loser in each round... slowest one to down their pint, has to neck a pint of piss...not any old piss, their own piss! What a bloody laugh it was.'

'Did you...?'

'Course, yea...bit of a beery taste if you must know. Not surprising I suppose.'

'And is this how the Marines, sorry, your famous Royal Marines, welcome guests...and gets recruits...is this how you were entertained over the weekend?'

'You don't get it Baz...they're fucking hard, have to be...we were up at 5.45... doin' warm up exercises before a short run, couple of miles...then breakfast... then learning how to do the assault course, part of which is under bleeding water...so did swimming training...oh and rifle range...that was after lunch... on and on it went...totally knackering. Work hard, play hard, is what they say... bloody elite lot, Marines. Top fucking fighters, world beaters you know ...they take on secret commando missions. Any road you should hear what they get up to.'

Tony supplied too many gruesome details involving the endurance and infliction of pain, lots of blood, guts, and torture, though he didn't use that word, instead describing it as effective interrogation techniques.

To change the subject someone made the comment: 'So...you have to be incredibly superhuman fit then?'

'You bet. Understatement mate. Training is a killer, over thirty weeks ...loads don't make it, drop out. We did a lot of PE on the second day. The trainers they really push you, harder and harder. They kept saying: 'It's all a question of mind over matter. We don't mind...you don't matter!'

After Tony left, one of us, it was probably me, put on a posh fruity voice: 'My dears, I do declare, it's perfectly charming what these navy chappies get up to in the mess.'

Anyway, that was more or less how I remember the conversation going when I think back over those five long decades. It left an indelible impression on me, I don't know if it was the same for the others who had heard him that day. The whole business had come as a surprise to us, his fellow sixth formers. Although the end of our schooling was only three or four months away, quite a few of us were settled on going to university, or one of the new polytechnics, the rest were aiming to start a job or an apprenticeship leading to a steady, safe career.

Our town was reasonably prosperous, or at least not in an area of deprivation. The point is that we could never imagine spending a long weekend near a Devon seaside town being ordered about by sadistic sergeant-major types. Not our scene at all and a completely alien experience I'm sure for most late teens at the end of the 1960s, beginnings of 1970s. What made it even stranger was the enthusiasm expressed by Tony for this bizarre choice. He had never shown much interest in anything before. Nothing in his family background to suggest the military. He had never joined cubs, scouts, cadets or even shown any interest in team games.

Tall, beefy, literally looking down his nose at us, and stocky. A large, lazy lump of lard, someone said.

I suppose you could say he was just a very cynical person, content with regularly making snidey remarks, sometimes witty though often wounding. The latter meant he was tolerated by others in our sixth form, not popular, and took it upon himself to attach himself to me when I moved to the school aged fourteen. I reckon now that he actually rather despised us all, but hid it well. Yes, I'm sure that was it.

'That bird you were with on Saturday, looks like her head's been squashed in a vice. Ugly gob on 'er. Like a post-box. I'd post a card telling her not to smile, when she does it's a right turn-off.' One typical string of remarks I remember. The other was that puerile pun he made, fortunately after the turbaned passer-by was out of earshot. We were with my Dad walking away from a football match. My Dad gave him a withering look. I didn't know what to say. My Dad told him to cut it out, he was very much a live-and-let-live sort of bloke.

The first time Tony went on about the Asian lack of taste, I had to admit, no, I hadn't noticed. When I asked what he meant by it, well it included every-thing that they ate, which was a surprise because curry and chips was already becoming very popular with the rest of us, especially after a few pints. I liked the colourful saris. He thought them silly. It was all so tacky and tasteless, according to him. He would mutter that they bought their trashy glad rags from filthy market stalls, still sweaty and smelly from their mates who made them. How they dressed, especially the shiny clothes, the plastic shoes, the gaudy jewellery, he despised. The crap cars they drove certainly did not meet Tony's approval either.

When at work many years later we had to undergo multicultural aware-ness along with endless health and safety training and customer care courses, I often thought of Tony. Of course I'd heard plenty of downright, outright racist comments in pubs and clubs and when my work took me into factory floors and canteens. At some football matches it could be sickening. Was Tony racist? Or was it social snobbishness? Didn't he think they might not want to buy leather shoes on religious grounds, or drive better cars, if they could afford it? Also, like us in our part of town, most of them didn't actually own a car.

There wasn't much talk or presence at our school of the Asian commu-nity, but what comments were made were like Tony's closed outlook, usually unpleasant and concluded with, 'they should all go back to where they came from'. It made my hometown feel pretty backward and provincial I can tell you.

However, the chapter in my maths textbook on Matrices claimed that, 'By indirection, find directions out'. That remark of Shakespeare's has meant more to me than anything else that followed in the rest of that chapter, so I failed 'O' Level Maths, but I mention this now because of how I found an opening, a new direction.

It happened that one day in our history lessons we had a bearded, hip student teacher doing his teaching practice. He kept saying to us: think for yourself; argue with what you're told; question things you read, things you're being told; don't be dummies; read a range of papers, of different political views. It was a shaft of sunlight opening up straight into our dull routine of taking endless notes from dreary old Mogsy. He was there, still in charge and when supervising the trainee kept muttering things like: 'They're not in the snug now you know, we don't want silly pub arguments here Mr Smedley!'

During Mr Smedley's stay with us, one Saturday, heading down to the market, I was passing the poor bloke who always stood there in all weathers trying to flog 'Socialist Worker' to the passing reluctant, unheeding masses. I stopped for once and thought, why not? Five pence, I think it was, exchanged for a copy of the paper and a big grin from the delighted seller.

Before I went home, I dropped into the library, found a comfy chair and examined the contents. Pretty dull, heavy going, except for an article all about immigration. It even mentioned our town. Fifty years is plenty of time to forget all the fine detail, but the core message I do recall was to not let the boss class divide and rule. It's all a class issue at heart it said. The term 'scapegoat' was used a lot. I remember there was very little footie news or rock music in it. I left the paper in the library, but borrowed its main message on immigration.

Back now to today. I noticed the squaddies on board our train were not all, as it had first appeared, loud-mouthed yobs. A couple were far more restrained. The guy opposite me spoke with a lovely West Country burr, and catching his eye I thought I could detect a sensitive young man. I may have been imagining it, but I thought he almost looked embarrassed by the conduct of his colleagues.

Away on my left the quietest member of the whole brothers in arms was a tall, handsome black guy. What was noticeable was that when he spoke there was considerable respect and attention paid to him, to what he said, which wasn't much, but it carried weight with the others. He, Dom, was the oldest. This point was demonstrated to everyone within earshot, so most of the carriage, after they had held an animated discussion with Army ID cards shown to prove this fact. Then something was said by Dom's immediate neighbour that jumped out at me:

'If you lot think Worcester's a shithole you should try Harrogate. Me and Dom went when we was at camp down there...in that town every bugger stares at you. Ignorant bleeders. Worse for you Dom weren't it.'

'Yea...I felt like I was bein' judged...like all the time.'

I suddenly remembered from over fifty years ago something that wise old Les Mappin our Art teacher had said about the rational survival fear of the stranger. Perhaps deep within us from primitive times we still carried a hint of anxiety about those who looked different, but surely it was high time we should and could grow out of this as it wasn't helpful now to our chance of survival?

Two steps forward, one step back? I was a social worker supporting young people with disabilities and difficulties into work and it made me think of all the debates we used to have concerning cultural awareness, discrimination, equal opportunities, race and class. Sorry, I digress.

Tony always dressed smartly, had a neat, school-approved hairstyle and was revolted by my mate Nigel, who to escape the school rule about hair length, which must be above the collar at the back and no longer than mid-ear at the side profiles, only washed his locks on a Friday night ready for letting it all hang out at the weekend. During school days Nigel's heavily greasy matted hair was plastered back behind his ears and somehow hidden, scrunched down inside his collar.

The nearest Tony came to admitting our hip psychedelic, protesting, happening times and allowing it to seep into his world was when he bought Dylan's 'Self-portrait', famously reviewed by our bible, Rolling Stone magazine, in terms of: 'What is this shit?' He then asked to borrow my 'Blonde on Blonde' and merely found that masterpiece totally bemusing.

Thinking about it, his close friendship with me has to be considered odd. I remember feeling uncomfortable at times. In many ways we were polar opposites. Physically, I could if I wanted, hide behind him being so tiny and thin and he such a hefty lump. I struggled with the schoolwork, he managed with an absolute minimum of effort to coast along. You see I'm still trying to fathom him out.

We did share a similar social background, living in parallel streets of Victorian terrace houses set in the grid of a dozen or so near the High Street. It would be accurate to describe my background and Tony's as lower middle class. His house interior was so similar to mine that we could have swopped and any difference hardly noticed, right down to the dark brown carpet in the back living room and a similar lino pattern in the kitchen. Our front rooms were only entered into when our parents had guests, so hardly ever used. His old man was a junior clerk in some office in town and his mother, before children arrived worked on the very same post-office counter my father occupied for forty-five long years. Tony too had one younger brother and sister, in that order. Boys in one bedroom, our sisters stuck in the box rooms. We never spoke of them.

One big difference though was my mother being a Roman Catholic. A devout one at that. After Tony's second away weekend with the Royal Marines he told me:

'They don't fuck about you know, the Marines, not like the regular army... that Bogside riot, a bloody battle it was really...it would have all been over in ten minutes if we'd been let in...this Marine commander bloke was telling us... would have wiped out the mad Micks once and for all. Wouldn't have taken any shit from them. Then we'd go and get those IRA bastards...can't wait to put an end to 'em.'

I couldn't understand how Tony could be so mindless. I found it scary, deeply depressing and most of all downright offensive hearing him mouthing this disgusting garbage. At that time my mum was cheering on Bernadette

Devlin and the Civil Rights Movement as we watched the news. She would explain to us exactly why. Her da had been a proud Nationalist, a true Republican. Later, as a student, I learnt that Republicans can be divided into two types: the revolutionary activists, with a few justifying the use of violence; the vast majority, far more passive, patient constitutionalists prepared to wait for a united Ireland to come to pass, peacefully. If I had known that at the time would I have been able to persuade Tony to...? No, that's wishful thinking. His mind was completely locked. He had his calling, a true vocation.

You see I am searching to find, by interrogating my memory, why Tony and I turned in such different directions on leaving school. I took a year out. You might say I dropped out, to find myself or something. I bummed around a bit, thumbing my way here and there. I found a commune squatting in Bristol and tried that for a few weeks. Someone asked me would I like to go and live in France on a barge where she had friends. I declined. I did find myself, man, in a way. What I found out was that I preferred a bit more security, some boundaries to the freedom I had imagined would suit me. I took flight from the freedom I had found in the alternative lifestyle and applied for university.

I did meet up with Tony once more before I headed off to be a full-time student. Better described as an encounter at a crowded party. He was sat in a corner, a young woman firmly ensconced in his lap despite his bandaged, injured ankle. The injury he was carrying was the reason he was back with his parents on leave for a couple of weeks. He'd twisted it very badly during a training exercise. He was shaven-headed, in sharp contrast to my shoulder-length hair and beard. He did exchange a few words with me, spoken very quietly and without any hint of genuine interest. I couldn't help noticing though the adoration in his companion's eyes. Clearly, he was of overwhelming interest to her, a home-grown hero back from the wars. A man for clear-cut action, leaving the rest of us partygoers as people with only dopey far out ideas. Whereas to command or be commanded was now his whole world.

We were always being told by those in authority that we should look up to and admire people like Tony as there he was doing his duty defending us all, night and day.

Eight years later, in 1980, I was back at my parents for the weekend and idly picking up the local rag to glance through it, I suddenly noticed a big headline that made me shout out, like the young these days, OMG.

'LOCAL ROYAL MARINE KILLED, tragic helicopter training exercise'.

Tony, a Lieutenant Commander, along with two other Lieutenant Commanders, was killed in a training exercise off Cape Wrath in Scotland. The report said he was twenty-seven years old, married with two young daughters. I read and re-read. How strange, how our lives had turned out. His was already over.

Last week, I had a look online and found a photograph showing his name, rank and dates carefully chiselled on a swish gravestone, a large, plain-grey slab.

In Memory

I couldn't possibly have guessed what I would find when I heaved open the door of that church. That ancient holy place in Wales. A tiny structure, surrounded by sky, sitting quietly on the hillside with only the sound of the sea crashing way down below as company. A place that meant so much to both of us.

I returned there recently and had a nasty, unexpected shock. It was a strange business altogether. Let me tell you about it because I keep trying to imagine what you would have felt, would have thought, and what you would have done if you were me. Afterall you would quite often take a view that surprised and intrigued me.

Over the years I'd read about grief. Not in a deliberate, intentional way, but with you being nearly five years older than me, I probably thought about it a little more than most. I paid attention when the topic cropped up in newspaper features, in conversation, or sometimes in the novels I read. What would it feel like? What would the hit be like? Impossible to know while you and I were still alive. Rather like, for me, never knowing what it felt like to be pregnant and giving birth.

The day I set off on my journey back there began as every day must. For ten years now I've been following exactly my same early-morning routine. In the days after your funeral, I held on to the stage directions grimly, and still replay the scene every single morning, an instinctive performance with familiar props. I needn't rehearse all the details for you now, I'm certain you could recite them without any prompting. The result of all this helps me to arise and carries me downstairs without a stumble in thought or deed. You'd be glad to hear that I enjoy the same substantial breakfast. I almost feel I do so in remembrance of you, of us.

To be honest, I had been delaying the trip to visit our church for years. I had placed high hopes that we could somehow reconnect there, that you would be present in some form, however fleeting or flimsy. My sentimental, clinging feeling, which I couldn't shake off, was that if I put in enough effort, had the necessary willpower and genuine faith, something significant would happen. Wishful thinking? All nonsense? Yet I kept telling myself, it could happen. The place either did retain something special of ours, something of us, or it didn't. I ought to find out.

So you see, there was a lot riding on making this visit to our joyful place. I had checked that the church would be open during the day, adopting your sensible approach, and the website even informs you how to contact the key holders if required.

Mid-morning, I stepped off the low kerb out onto St Peter's Square, its long forgotten church demolished over a hundred years ago, and walked across what was part of the Peterloo massacre field. Scan left, look right, look left again. So many Metro lines are scored into the surface of the square. Perhaps even more now than in your time. Trams constantly approach or recede it seems. Pedestrians criss-cross in front of you. Many talk on phones to that unseen cloud of callers. Deliveroo deliverers chicane past at speed. Mind those dog leads. That buggy. And the trailing, rumbling suitcases on wheels. That day I set off to Wales I felt almost safely on the Central Library shore when suddenly, from nowhere, two mounted police appeared bearing down on my starboard bow. Well, at least I had noticed the skateboarder in time to pause and let her fly past. Wait till the electric scooters proliferate I thought. I missed your hand to hold.

You know I used to admire and envy your upright posture and easy walking style, lovely to watch when my gait's so rickety. I dreaded seeing our reflection in a store window where I was the crooked man walking a crooked mile beside you, trying not to lurch into you or confuse oncoming pedestrians. You used to patiently explain they were often fooled by my upper body appearing to move in the opposite direction to my legs. They had done their best, the medics, with various procedures in my early years, patched me up so I could enjoy cricket and tennis.

On the train I sit facing forwards. Suddenly, we're in a tunnel, not a long one, but time enough to take me back in an instant to St Ninian's cave, Isle of Whithorn, Kirkcudbrightshire. Over thirty years ago we camped nearby. Our children enjoyed searching for crabs and taking fright, or screaming with delight when large ones scuttled towards them. As the train hurtles and rattles its way through the dark, I picture again the shingle shore that leads to the cave. The children enjoyed exaggerating the scrunching sound of their marching footsteps. We remembered best the pair of peregrines floating aloft the cliff tops searching for prey. The cave held the sound of pounding waves, remorselessly recording each moment of time passing, yet promising all is timeless. In contrast to the cold eyes cast by the falcons, out at sea were mild-eyed seals bobbing about, appearing and disappearing as they pitched and rolled in the lively sea.

In a whoosh, blinking, we arrive into daylight, the tunnel gone. St Ninian, it is said, retreated to the cave to pray and meditate. They say he was concerned to learn how best to preach salvation. How on earth do they know, you would have said?

So much we held dear is slipping away from me. No pockets in shrouds they say in Oldham, you don't take owt with you when you go. To think though that all traces of our treasure trove of shared experience, the trivial as well as the profound, is lost overboard when we walk the plank and sink beneath the waves. We will become only what others remember of us, and even that slides slowly or rapidly away, fading completely with the passing generations.

Before long, after leaving the tiny station, I am sitting in my B and B room, less fun than a campsite, but more comfortable for my creaking joints. Tomorrow I'll wend my way through the woods, up over the mountain's lower shoulder and enter our church once again. Will something at least poetical occur? Remember Lydia, our old friend? Whenever she felt in a rut or low she would declaim: 'Run up the sail, set out to sea comrades'. Some poem or other she'd done at school. Something about new starts, seeking adventure and self-discovery.

Out from town I found the footpath I wanted, went past the farmhouse we admired, then found the lane that slouches down between banks of hawthorn. A quarter mile further on the climb is up into the woods and along an ancient path cut into the steep hillside. Stunted oaks tumble down on the left and strain up on my right to cover the hillside, all slanting stiffly towards the ground as if caught in mid-collapse. Lichen clings on every limb, each stone caressed. Dankness pervades, a haven for eerie fungi. The pungent plainchant incense of ransoms fills the air. Tongue-shaped ferns begin to appear as I edged out of the unspoken melancholy into sunshine and meadows and began the demanding final ascent. A profusion of purple willow herb filled my eyes. Masses of mesmerising orange butterflies settled, restlessly alighted, and resettled endlessly repeating their fluttering moves.

The church was my destination. I sweated up the path on my pilgrimage. More sheep farms and houses dotted about the hillsides as I started to smell and hear the sea. I remember thinking I'll soon be under the skeletal roof ribs within the stubborn stone walls, a Jonah swallowed up by an ossified whale. I felt the strong pull of the thirteenth century and smiled at the thought. Not all is entirely transient then. This place of grace remains, lingers on. Some are puzzled by the persistence of faith. The seeking since childhood to understand the big picture.

Ten minutes later, I stood outside the low door, paused and leaning heavily on the door, entered. I was greeted by the overwhelming stink of dope. Heavy, sticky dozy dope. I felt dizzy, disoriented. Our lovely church, our haven, our little fortress, stank to high heaven of skunk. Mirth and mumbling emerged from the shadows near the tiny font.

I stopped in my tracks, stood and stared. Gobsmacked. I do remember taking a couple of strides forward to try and see... and saw a couple of lads splayed out on pews, legs and arms askew, dangling all over the place. One was gazing at me, smirking. I wanted to shout. I needed to scream, but what, I didn't know. I froze again. I felt tears coming. A lot of tears coming very fast.

I turned and fled. Rushed back out of the church. I needed you. I staggered over to sit down against a gravestone. I sat there numb for I don't quite know how long.

I regained some sense of what had happened and where I was. I decided to play a waiting game. Surely they'd soon go? I thought to stand up but a figure emerging from out the porch made me pause. One of the youths. He ambled over towards the old yew in the corner, turned his back to the church and me and had a piss, I presume. Then turned, settled his trousers, looked around and saw me. I was rooted to the spot, totally transfixed by the sight of him coming towards me along the path. He stood hovering over me, looking tall and spindly as I felt myself shrinking back, curling up.

'Well...hello matey...gave you a bit of a turn back there did we?', he muttered.

'No worries...not after anything off you...only wanna see if you're ok...an' what you doing here, like?'

I found my voice, but not how to use it fully to explain myself.

'I'm...I came to...ugh...well, find out something...someone...some special...'

He grinned. Then plonked himself down alongside me.

'Me too...An' we never seen any bod up here, that's sort of what we like... anyroad you found us...and we can't be special coz you fucked off real quick like.'

'Sorry...if I appeared rude...such a shock...I've never seen anyone here before either and...'

'Yea...chill mate...no worries...just...chill.'

'How do you mean, what...?'

'See...ugh...maybe you did right...seeing us is scallies...we be real bad news, or Tex is, my mate like. I tells 'im don't toke in the bloody church. Says he needs the holy weed...real cool vibe in there.'

'How do you mean you're bad news?'

'Ha...huh...that would be telling. It's true like. Tex he...he's a criminal, mind.'

'And this church is a sort of...hideout then?'

This caused him to snigger, then slur: 'Sor' of...you could say, yea.'

By now I appreciated that this guy was not very intoxicated. In my time working in prison education I knew not to enquire into the exact nature of an inmate's misdemeanours, but also knew that some who were serving time want to tell you all about it, either because they feel that they have been a victim of a miscarriage of justice or simply because they think it will impress you. A few simply want to act hard.

'It's like this see...Tex come up here to do his payback thing...you know...so he don't pay no big fine like or waste time in the fucking nick. He quite liked cutting the grass, hated weeding for hours...But he does like it up here see... says you're left in peace, feel calm...an' we can meet some birds, well one from the farm down there an' her mate...she was at school with us see.'

'So he...Tex...comes up here quite a bit with you?'

'Oh yea. We get a train from Towyn...we got special tickets, like. A free pass you might say...Anyhow we need to get away a bit from Towytown...Tex gets into bother see...with this Chink... chippy shop like...bugger gives us too much grief...says no can vape ciggies in my shop...no sale...money not regal...fake note...no argue, you out my shop! So Tex yells at him ...don't fucking mess with us Chinky...givus our curry an' chips or I'll fuckin' do you damage...an screams plenty more stuff like that...an' then it were said he was all racialistic an' all that...giving out abuse...coz of what Tex said like...an' he went back day after and says more of the same...Chink got police...we ran off but people in queue grassed...wanna see him taken down.'

'So no more Chinese food for you two, or do you go elsewhere?'

'There is another Chinky chippy in Towyn...but...he effing hates 'em all, they can keep their bleeding chow and choppysticks he says, stick it up where the sun don't shine...so he's stuffed...'

'But not with chips...Why you telling me all this?'

'Well, I'm saying soz I suppose...Tex reckons he's dead hard an' wants everyone to know. Smokes dope all day long...his dim Da' got him started like... made him a right dead dopehead I reckon. His Mam walked out. Then the bugger got expelled. He ain't much fun no more.'

'But...well I'm still not sure why you're telling me all this?'

'Well, like I say...I am sorry we freaked you out, but it's our place too you know...I feel it's cool here, can be ya'self an makes me feel a better pers...oh I dunno, can't say why...Chill.'

'In what way different?'

'Can't say...Look thing is, I've had enough of 'im...Where you from mate? Got wheels...parked at the farm?'

'No car. I came from Manchester on the train.'

'Oh well...other thing is...best to warn you...don't go back in there...and he may come out ...if he can get to his feet. Anyway, I'm off...had enough.'

'Warn me...What d'ya mean?'

'Tex...he's screwed up big...bit of a maniac.'

'Yea ok...so you say you've had enough of him?'

'Yea...sod tells me Megan's mate Sue will meet us yea...but now he just said, oh soz, meant to tell ya...ugh...she can't come...reckon he knew full well like before we sets off...bloody liar!'

At this point, he stood up. I too got up from the hard ground. I reckoned he'd completed what he wanted to say, and sure enough, after he'd smiled and said, 'Anyway, I'll keep coming here...great place to chill', strode off.

No point hanging around the church I thought, especially as I'd noticed a tiny figure far below inching along the path that brings you up here. Probably Tex's date. The notion of a date, in the traditional sense, with Tex, made me almost laugh out loud. I wouldn't know what to say to her, if anything, so I turned away and instinctively climbed over the low wall of the graveyard towards the cliff edge.

As I did so, I felt strangely liberated, released from the shock encounter in the church. It had served a useful service...silly to think my love for you could only ever be contained or felt in this one building, just waiting for me to return. Or found by reliving or trying to recreate the past. I can find you present anywhere, anytime and that's always been the case. Apart from me, but still a part of me.

I gazed out over the vast expanse of the bay. The sweep and curve were pleasantly familiar and comforting because you are sitting beside me silently drinking in the sheer enormity of the vastness on show of sea and sky with a horizon that beckons us into the beyond. It's even wider and lonelier without you, but I'm glad now I came. I thought about what the young man had said, an unexpected conversation certainly, but welcome all the same, don't you think?

BV - #0073 - 210524 - C0 - 210/148/6 - PB - 9781912710607 - Matt Lamination